# Summer Haven

Published by:
Powder River Publishing LLC
1014 Black Mountain Road
Thermopolis, Wyoming 82443

Copyright © 2025
ISBN: 978-1-956881-60-8
Printed in the United States of America

We are a flash of fire—a brain, a heart, a spirit. And we are three-cents-worth of lime and iron—which we cannot get back.

—**Thomas Wolfe, Look Homeward Angel**

# Prologue

During the summer of 1970, a time when I and all my buddies in college were wondering how we were going to get rid of Richard Nixon before he had the opportunity to send us all off to Viet Nam to die, I got lucky and drew a high-enough draft number in the lottery to where I considered myself safe from having to participate in possible future jungle combat, so I stayed safe and sound in school and worked during the summer at Summer Haven Cemetery outside the city of Athens, Tennessee to make enough money to pay for tuition and board the next two years at the University of Tennessee-Chattanooga. I spent two summers at Summer Haven welding a pick and a shovel and driving around on riding mowers and golf carts and spending the days cutting grass and pulling weeds and over time even becoming somewhat of an expert at manning a shovel and digging and filling in graves. It was hard work, but I grew to enjoy being outside in the meadow-like atmosphere of the grounds instead of having to work cooped up in a store or a restaurant or outside paving highways in the hot sun like a lot of my friends were unlucky enough to be doing. Most of the day I was sheltered by the huge old trees that grew on the cemetery grounds and revel in the breezes that blew on my body through the shaded lanes that ran up and down the two mile cemetery grounds. Lots of times I would finish up my assigned duties in the afternoon and have some leisurely minutes to lean back in my mower or cart and observe the scenes that surrounded me. I could watch squirrels race around the ground and scamper up trees, check out hawks soaring overhead looking for prey, view the wildlife that made its home there away from the suburbs that surrounded the property, and take in the many headstones and gravesites that were around everywhere I looked. I made it a habit those days to carry a cooler around with water and ice and a couple of bologna sandwiches on white bread to eat daily for my lunch, and while I chewed my meal and cooled my heels at noon or the late afternoons each day I found myself falling into the habit of reading names and dates of births and deaths and making up stories in my head about the dead souls who were buried around me. After two years of this practice, I found myself so enthralled in these customary reposes that I carried the tradition with me into my adult years, making it somewhat of a compulsory point to visit the graveyards of whatever town I happened to be in on trips or vacations and check out who exactly was reposing there. I guess it could be said I grew so entrenched in my morbid hobby that it appeared to my friends and family down through the years I was more interested in the dead and gone than I ever had been with any of the living I walked and worked among.

The truth is I was never much of a traveler, so I never visited that many cities or checked out too many unfamiliar graveyards outside of Summer Haven. I tended to stay home and watch television when I wasn't working at my job with the realty company examining new and old houses up for sale and getting my team of laborers to whip them into salable shape, painting, sanding, removing the old and bringing in the new, but there came a time now and again when I would grow bored of my workday surroundings and my pedestrian life and make a visit to Summer Haven for a while just to re-imagine a new story or two in my head. There was something about the place that certainly beat the usual tedium of the work week all to hell, or at least it was that way to me. It was like when I visited Summer Haven someone there always had something to say, and I was more than willing to listen.

# MEDITATION HILL

## Bette Marie Chandler
## Beloved Wife and Mother
## (1947- 2022)

**N**ow the main thing to know about me is I was never really sick a day of my life, and the only reason I'm here today is because I came down with Alzheimer's and dementia right after I turned 72, just after I retired from teaching First Grade for 50 years at Mc-Minn County Elementary, up on the ridge where Eddie and I had our farm. The Alzheimer's came on me so fast I didn't have time to prepare for it at all; one minute I was happy and looking forward to retirement so I'd have more time to see my grandkids and help out at the church, and then almost overnight it was like a big fog came over me and I couldn't hardly remember what I'd done the past fifteen minutes or where I was right then or what I'd been doing before I had to stop and wonder why I was feeling so doggoned lost all of a sudden.

I put it down for a while to just the simple fact that I was getting old and forgetful like most everybody does, and that because I was having trouble remembering things was because I had lived so many years by then that my poor old brain just didn't have enough room left inside it to house any more additional information, so naturally some stuff had to be pushed out of there in order to make room for something else. I tried telling myself it was as simple as all that until I started realizing that, no, there wasn't any additional information or knowledge coming into my head and pushing old stuff away, but it was more like the data I didn't have stored anymore was gone from me for good and there didn't seem like much of a way of ever getting it back, and nothing was coming in to replace

3

it, and all that was happening was my mind seemed to be shrinking and capable only of holding a few things at a time and the cupboard and storage bin was getting smaller every day. Soon I got to where I didn't know I'd forgotten anything to begin with, and all my friends and family began being strangers to me and my first impulse when I saw them was to be afraid and think of trying to defend myself, because it started becoming really evident to me that maybe they meant to do me harm.

I think I trusted Eddie the most, I guess because his face looked familiar to me some days, and he brought me food and helped me take a bath for a while, but then it got to the point where everybody looked the same and I just learned to smile back at them and act like what they said made sense, and the last thing I truly recall was wondering what my name was and how I ever got to the place I was in to begin with.

That's the way it works on you, you know. You forget how to think and you don't know who you are and the last thing that comes along is you forget how to eat, and the sad thing about that is you don't even know it when it happens. You just get weaker and weaker and then your body gives out and you're gone.

I don't remember anything for the longest time until I one day came back to myself and I was here at Meditation Hill and I somehow knew my body was here in the ground beneath the marker and it didn't take a genius from that point to figure out I was dead. At first I was really sad and wanted to spend eternity crying about my fate, but slowly it came to me that I was where I was and there wasn't anything I could do about it until I got called to Heaven by God—I hope there's a Heaven and there's a God, I think there is, but I just haven't got to that stage yet—and it didn't take but a little bit before I learned I didn't have to just stay trapped inside my coffin for any undetermined length of time, but that I had the power of freedom to mosey about and look around and take in the cemetery sites and see the birds and the trees and such, and after I got accustomed to that I learned I could just will myself to be someplace back among those who were still alive, Eddie and my children and my grandkids and my sister and all them, and I could go look in on friends and see what they were doing and maybe find out if any of them missed me or not. I didn't look too close and tried not to get upset and hold a grudge against anybody if it seemed like they weren't the worse for wear that I wasn't around anymore; no, I just tried to understand that the living couldn't help themselves if they didn't continually concentrate on those who had passed, that it's not natural for anybody to grieve that way for so long, that people had to get on with their lives after a while and keep on going until their own time came, and once I started thinking that way I was all right. I was my good old sweet self again.

Because, you see, I may not have been the prettiest girl around when I was in my flower, eighteen, nineteen, twenty, but I could put a good case forward that I was the one with the happiest heart. I didn't bear anyone any malice no matter what they did or said or thought about me. I may have been overweight and not as financially well-off as a lot of girls in my class, but it can at least be said that I never had an unkind word for anyone and I smiled and laughed my way through a lot of things that would have made a sweet chariot full of preachers shake their fists to the skies and curse God for all they were worth over.

I guess the thing that intrigues you so much—at least in my case—is when you pass over you have so much time and you're capable of doing and remembering anything. The funniest things began coming to me after such and such a time. It wasn't so much about Eddie or my family or friends or people at the church who I had been around for so long, but it was those things that just happened once or twice and then were gone never to come back again, and me, when I was alive, I accepted that kind of thing pretty easily, but now, since I have all day and night for I don't know how long to come, there's plenty of time for even the vaguest of memories to come into my head, and it seems like I can go on forever calling them up and seeing them again like they were just happening for the first time.

I got to thinking about Tommy Blackburn one of those times.

Tommy was this boy I knew from church. He was a year younger than I was and he went to a different school than I did, but he and his family started coming to our church when I was about thirteen and he was twelve. He had an older brother who I thought was really cute and his daddy was really handsome with just the bluest eyes this side of Paul Newman, so I didn't pay a whole lot of attention to Tommy much there at the start. He was just this skinny little kid and twelve years old, so why should I have?

But it turned out Tommy's big brother wasn't nothing but a hood and mean to boot, and he for sure didn't have any interest in a fat girl like me, and Tommy's father worked some kind of job where he was away on weekends most of the time, so most of the time Tommy's brother quit coming to church and it was just Tommy and his mother, and Tommy got to where he was popular with everybody and good friends with my best friend Linda's little brother and we'd all end up at Linda's house together at the same time. So, between being at Linda's and being at church every Sunday, it got to where Tommy and I knew each other pretty well. We were in the same youth group together and we'd go on retreats and attend church camp for four or five years in a row, and being as I was pretty popular too because of my personality and ability to laugh and get along with others, after a while there was a bunch of us kids from church who were good friends together and did everything as a big group all the time outside of church, and Tommy and I were right there in the center of that group. This went on all the way through high school and into our first years of college.

What I remember so much and what I dwelled on for a long time as I became accustomed to my new surroundings at Summer Haven was that July night in 1969 when it became clear to me that Tommy Blackburn and I were never going to advance to the stage where we were a couple, which surprised me that the answer came to me so clear and undeniable, since up until that time I'd found myself very slowly starting to fall in love with this boy who was younger than me and only a rising sophomore in college, this boy who was not ready to settle down in one way or another.

Tommy and his male friends were all at the age where they wanted to be wild and have fun anytime they could get away with it. There were maybe six boys altogether, and over the last couple of years it became apparent to anybody who was paying attention that these guys lived for the nights when they could get someone to buy them illegal alcohol or when one of them could get lucky enough to come across a bag of marijuana and they could get drunk or high or both and blast out music riding around in somebody's car, laughing and doing ridiculous things and attempting perilous feats none of them would even think of trying in their right mind in the light of day. I wasn't there, but I heard tell of Tommy diving off a bridge to cool himself off and landing in about a foot worth of creek water. If he hadn't been intoxicated I'm certain he would have killed himself.

But I was home on that July 20th night when Tommy and Lawrence Briggs came by in Tommy's Chevrolet. They had a paper bag filled with beer they'd procured somewhere, and they knocked on my door and wanted to know if I was going to watch the moon walk. I'd forgotten all about the men landing up there and how they were going to show them on TV setting foot on the moon's surface—don't ask me why. I guess I just was thinking about a lot of different things right then and it just slipped my mind how history was fixing to be made. My mother and dad had gone off somewhere earlier, probably to watch the moon walk themselves at some friends, and my big brother was out somewhere too, so I let Tommy and Lawrence in and turned on the TV in the living room so we could sit on the couch and watch it all happen together.

At first I thought that we'd all be overwhelmed and mystified by what was transpiring before us, and in some part of me I thought maybe this was the night when Tommy and I would come together like I had this feeling we were going to someday, that maybe all it took was for mankind to do something unheard of and special like walk on the moon which nobody ever dreamed was such a thing that might actually happen, and maybe if miracles like that came to fruition then perhaps it wasn't so impossible for me to find a dream fellow of my own, instead of watching every other girl in my path have it happen to them but never to me. I wondered if this July 20th in the year of 1969 was going to go down as one of those fantastically unbelievable nights in the history of mankind and the world and that Tommy and I might fall in love until death did us part on this very same evening.

Tommy and Lawrence never would shut up and listen to what Chet Huntley was saying on television. They were busy chugging beer and telling Helen Keller jokes and talking about these couple of girls they'd double-dated with the past weekend, and it was like I or Chet Huntley or David Brinkley weren't even there in the room, like it was no big deal if anybody walked on the moon or not, not as long as they could talk about how far they could go with some girl I'd never heard of or whether somebody's parents were going to be out of town anytime soon so they could take these girls over to somebody's house and get them drunk and screw them all night long.

It wasn't five minutes before Neil Armstrong was fixing to step out on the lunar surface that Tommy suddenly seemed to get more than his fill of beer, that it went down the wrong way or he'd had too much of it or what, but he suddenly was bolting toward my front door trying to get out on the porch and fiddling with the handle and trying to get outside as fast as he could. But he didn't make it. He was throwing up on the floor and himself before he could make it to the porch. I sat there listening to him be sick and heave and say, "Oh, God" a couple of times. Then I heard Neil Armstrong say "Here's one small step for man."

I looked at the screen and there Neil was, a fuzzy figure standing on soil I'd never seen before. And out on my porch Tommy was coughing and spitting and saying "Oh, God" over and over.

I guess Tommy was ashamed of himself, or he at least didn't want to return to the scene of his own ignobly. He never came to my house again, and it wasn't long before I figured I was too old to go to youth socials anymore and moved my letter to a church near school and started going there, hoping for a fresh start. God was kind to me then, for that's where I met Eddie. He was going to be a teacher too, on top of being a farmer and helping out on the family farm. He would graduate and go back to Athens to teach sixth grade and help out on the farm when he could, seeing how his parents were getting up there and he was their only child.

I didn't have to be a genius to know I should go with him.

And that was that. I had a happy life teaching kindergarten and being a farm wife, and I got to where I enjoyed the sight of seeing Eddie up on his tractor doing his farmer thing. After a while I thought he was the handsomest farmer in the world, or at least in the world I knew.

Love didn't come all at once for me, but it finally came.

And up until lately I don't think I ever gave Tommy Blackburn much thought at all, and generally that was only when I'd run into somebody from the old days at a funeral or by chance, and from time to time someone would mention how Tommy moved to Florida after graduation and went to work in a bar. As far as anyone knew he was still down there somewhere, but no one seemed to know what town he'd finally settled in.

# SERENITY MEADOW

## Grantland Trammell
## Rest in Peace
## (1922-1998)

**I** got home from the War and finished up my service with the Army in 1946. I can't lie and say I saw a whole lot of action during my time over in Europe, but I guess I did as much of my share as anybody. I wasn't in any real battles, but I was always stationed somewhere where my company was the next one to be called up to the lines, so I spent a lot of time worrying and thinking about how any day now the time might come for me to take a bullet or get caught up in an explosion or get taken prisoner by the Nazis or something terrible like that. I didn't have to participate in D-Day or be involved in any really horrible scenes, but I'll still say the stress and fear and uncertainty took a toll on me just like it did everybody else. I lived on the cusp for more than a year, and after that long a time being in limbo it was hard to imagine that the War was some-day going to be over and I would make it back to the states alive and in one piece.

But I did make it through. When I got my discharge I was get-ting close to being 25 and had to decide whether I wanted to take the G.I. Bill and go to college or if I wanted to take a job and get started learning a trade. It wasn't like I had anyone much to advise me; my dad had died when I was eleven and all I had was a school-teacher big sister and my mother who was dying from diabetes by the time I got back. I never did have too many close friends growing up, because most of the time any friends I had in school ended up not liking me much. I had a quick temper and tended, I guess, to brood too much and hold a grudge when I thought somebody had

10

done something to me. I look at things now and I have to admit that maybe there was something wrong with me psychologically that I never learned to deal with. I couldn't seem to make or keep a friend, and I didn't have much luck in ever finding a girlfriend either, which to be honest was never. I never had a steady girl friend at all by the time I got back home, which is not a good thing for a young man getting set to be five years short of thirty.

I'd done my fair share of day-dreaming though.

I remember being stationed in New York, waiting to be shipped across the Atlantic to England and to perhaps enter the fray, having it multiply in my mind every hour of the day that my fate was out of my hands now and there wasn't anything I could do to determine if I was going to ever come back or if I was going to die overseas. I was lonesome for my home state of Tennessee and for the United States already and I hadn't even left yet. The nearer I got to be loaded on a carrier or flown on a transport to a foreign country the more scared and fearful I became, and after I got to the absolute limit of being frightened for my life my feelings soon became overcome by a new emotion, the pervading feeling of loneliness in every step I took, in every breath and beat of my heart. I was going to go to a place where no one knew me and I knew no one, and I was going to possibly die a young man who had never had the chance to be a part of anything that went on in real life, to die at a tender age in life and never have the opportunity to experience love or know what it feels like to be immersed in such a strange and mystical emotion.

The orders finally came through and my company learned we would be shipping out on Sunday. We had three days to wait, but no one was granted any leave or time to go out into the city to see the sights and try and have a little fun, probably because the army was afraid some of us might take the opportunity to take off and go AWOL and run as far as we could to get away from what awaited us. We were confined to our base until time for us to leave, so there was a lot of time sitting around thinking or staring at a blank wall waiting for the worst to happen.

I guess the brass in charge felt sorry for us, seeing how we were sacrificial lambs getting ready to go to slaughter, so they tried to do something nice for us before it was time to go. We were treated to a concert on Friday night, a small token of respite to help us face the ordeal ahead.

They were bringing in Les Brown and his band to entertain us. Doris Day would be with them.

Doris Day was the girl we all dreamed about. When she sang "Sentimental Journey" it was like we were being visited by an angel from heaven.

I think of that night now and fast-forward forty years to where I'm standing behind the counter in my own little restaurant off Henderson Avenue. My wife is leaving for the day—I actually found someone who'd marry me, I've been married twenty years to her by then—and I'm prepared to sit through the afternoon hours and maybe catch some business from some folks in the neighborhood wanting a late lunch or from a few of the employees at the Kroger store across the road, who'll sometimes walk over on their hour for lunch and eat at one of my three tables, just to get away from the store and read a magazine or something. I'm not very friendly with too many of them and most don't ever say the first thing to me other than what they want to eat, but there was this one fellow who worked there who came pretty regularly to eat a cheeseburger special most days he worked, and he and I got to where we had a speaking relationship. He'd look at some of the pictures I had on the wall from the War and newspaper headlines about Kennedy getting assassinated and the Titanic sinking and we'd actually have conversations about them. I had an old jukebox in the corner and he'd always drop a quarter in and play three songs while he waited for his cheeseburger to get ready. He played Elvis and the Platters and Johnny Mathis a lot, and one day to my surprise he played both sides of a Doris Day 45 I had on there, "Sentimental Journey" and "It's Magic."

He had heard "Sentimental Journey" before—my dad used to really like it, he said—but he had never heard "It's Magic." He thought Doris Day sounded better back then than she did in the present day of the 80s. He'd seen her on her television show one night and that had been enough for him until now.

That's when I told him the story of hearing Doris sing on the Friday night before we shipped out to go fight the Germans, and how I'd listened to that sweet voice thinking the whole time that this might be the last snatch of music I'd ever hear, that the songs would be over and I'd be on my way and might soon be dead before a song ever started up again where I could listen to it. I told him how it was back then, how falling in love and being happy for the rest of your life seemed like something that wasn't ever going to happen in the world you knew at that moment in time.

Business wasn't very good after a while—I had a McDonald's and a Burger King pop up around me and that's where everybody tended to go—and when my rent got raised I decided to move somewhere else and try and make a go of it there. There weren't many prime locations and after another year I had to let the business go and take a job delivering produce to stores across the city and a few small places in nearby towns. It wasn't good money at all and my wife, Ruth, finally had to go back to work at the age of sixty-one, at the Kroger store close to where the restaurant had been. She got a position as a checker, but it was part-time work and required her to work nights to get her hours, so it got to where we didn't see each other much. Maybe this was good for us, since I started missing her on those nights when she had to work, and it came to me that I had feelings for her that went deeper than I'd imagined before. Or maybe it was just I was lonely sitting around the house after driving around in a truck all day going to places where nobody knew my name and I didn't know theirs. My son had graduated high school and joined the army the year before, so he wasn't around to talk to either, although we'd never had much to say to each other for a while until he left.

One night, I left the house and went and ate dinner at a Kentucky Fried Chicken. I ordered a dinner to go and decided to go by Kroger and take it to Ruth so she could eat something on her break.

I ran into Charles that night, the kid who used to come in and have his lunch and play the jukebox. He recognized me right off, and came over and shook my hand. He asked me if I'd been listening to Doris Day much lately.

I think about that at night sometimes. It wasn't long after that Ruth had a stroke and dropped dead one afternoon when she was getting ready to go to work. I was out on my job and didn't know a thing about it until I came home and found her on the bedroom floor. There was a message on our phone from Kroger, asking her if she was coming to work today, but I didn't call them back and let them know what happened. I had too much on my mind right then. I called 911 and the police and an ambulance came and took Ruth away, and I sat in the living room and tried to call my son and let the family and her friends know what had happened. I couldn't think of anybody to call for myself, so I went a couple of days until the funeral was over and Ruth was buried in a plot she owned by her parents and my son had gone back to his base in North Carolina. I called the Kroger store and asked if Charles was there. I didn't even know his last name. He wasn't there, but whoever was in the office gave me his number, something that would never happen in this day and age because of privacy issues.

I called and he didn't answer, but the answering machine came on and I tried to leave a message. I started crying and I don't know how clear the message came through. I was just talking and crying to the machine because I didn't have anywhere else to go or no one else to listen to me.

Charles never called me back. I kept thinking he would for a week or two, but I was almost glad he didn't, since I'd made such a fool out of myself and hadn't been able to face up to death the same way I had when it had scared me so much the night Doris Day sang to all us boys preparing to approach the end of our lives.

I didn't make it but a couple of more months after that. I guess I just couldn't cope with the way my life had turned out, and I drank a lot at night and ate lunch meat and potato chips all the time, and one afternoon I ran a red light in the truck and plowed into a milk truck. I was dead almost instantly and no one else was hurt, and for that I was glad. I didn't want to hurt anyone.

See, I was happy to be dead; it was the way I needed to be. That sounds awful, but it's true. I'd had the kind of life that I was glad to see it come to an end. I was glad to put it behind me.

# ROCKABYE VALLEY

## Melinda Joan Brewer
## Our Little Angel
## December 14-22, 2018

There's not too much to remember at all. All I recall was light and darkness and my mother's breast and my father in the background looking down. Sometimes he would hold me too. I would be in his arms. But it wasn't for long. I didn't even make it until Christmas. It wasn't even nine days I was alive. It's no wonder I don't suffer from the pangs of memory while I'm here, thinking about any of the good times that happened while I was a part of the world, because there just wasn't enough time to make any kind of memories of when I was around, because I left too soon for too much of anything to happen. I can barely remember my mother or father from back then, only coming to recognize them later when I was apart from them and able to see where I had come from and who I was kin to during that very short while I was alive. I look now and see my mother and think she is very pretty, and my father is a nice-looking man too, so it gives me pause and makes me wonder just how much I would have taken after either of them in a physical sense if I'd been around to do any growing up. I guess it's impossible to say, since I think the rules are I have to stay in my earthly form for a certain amount of time, and it could be I'll never see what I might have looked like if I had made it to kindergarten or high school or made it through college and married someone and became a mother myself. I guess there's just no way of knowing, and that's hard to take sometimes.

But there's good to it too, because at least I didn't have to spend countless hours growing up wondering why I wasn't as pretty as the next girl sitting in a desk beside me at school. That's the way it is with my big sister, Cathy, you know. She worries about that kind of stuff all the time. She's thirteen now—she was seven when I was born—and all she does is look in the mirror and wish she was someone else constantly. It's not that she's ugly or anything. Shoot, I can tell just by watching her the last six years that she's going to be okay in the end. She won't be the prettiest girl in her school but she won't look like a dead dog either. She'll have enough guys asking out on dates or wanting to take her to the prom and all that business, all that stuff I'm going to miss, whether it was going to be good or bad for me, so at least Cathy gets a chance to experience something, and if it was in my power I'd like to let her know that she ought to at least be thankful she's out there getting to do something. She's not stuck here in the Little Lamb section of Rockabye Valley with artificial flowers in a vase sitting on top of my name until the cows come home or Resurrection Day comes along and we all have a ticket to Heaven or wherever it is we're heading to spend eternity.

I guess that's the hardest part of it, though, the being here and thinking about all those things that might have happened if you hadn't had a bad heart and what you might have been when you grew up—just a bunch of questions that you'll never be able to answer. I was hoping that when I crossed over to where I am I'd be given a lot of answers to all my questions, but so far, after six years, I still don't know.

I guess what's really surprising about being here at Summer Haven is the fact that there's very little crying that goes on around my section. I suppose everyone who comes here can't help but bawl and wail for a while when they first get here, since everyone is so young and unknowledgeable of what is going on with them, but after a few hours it comes to you how there's no one coming to take you out of here or help you out or sing to you at night when it's time to go nighty-night. It's like a baby learns pretty fast and all on their own that this is where they are and are going to be and all the crying in the world isn't going to do a thing to change it. I even believe that after you get used to it and become accustomed to where your home is you automatically calm down and go to somewhere inside yourself where there's peace. It's not like you're altogether happy about what is going on, but it is that the bad stuff has begun to fade and it's all so quiet and calm and there's no more worry about what to eat or if someone is going to come and change you because you're wet and all that dependency rigmarole that babies are so thrust into right from the start, but soon you learn that all that worry has been eliminated and isn't there for you anymore, and you're all right here in this place, and that it's quiet and peaceful if you want it to be and there's music you can hear in your mind if you want. And if you lay very still and concentrate you will know what your mommy and daddy are doing at home with your sister, if they're sitting down to eat or going to church or going to bed for the night, or if it's a Sunday afternoon and they are coming by to visit and make sure the flowers on my grave are straight and the vase hasn't turned over.

Sometimes the wind blows pretty hard out here and wreaths and decorations fall down or get blown away.

It's not all the time, but sometimes the children do get lonely here and the silence gets to them a little, and that's when after the sun goes down and the moon comes up and there aren't any visitors coming around anymore that somebody will start singing a song, something like "Twinkle, Twinkle, Little Star" or "Jesus Loves Me" or something like that, and then other voices start joining in and pretty soon it's like a choir of us singing songs that only we can hear. Maybe some of the animals that live around here can hear us too, because a lot of times you can see an owl or a deer or even a fox come along and stop for a minute as if they're trying to decide if something is coming after them, but they end up staying around and listening like the sound of the children singing is making them peaceful too.

I don't mind nights like that at all. Sometimes it makes me glad that I'm here and not somewhere else, because I know that there are places away from here and back in the life from where I came from that are pretty bad.

Another thing that you have to get used to—and it gets bad at first and stays that way for a while—is the fact that after a time you start understanding that because you are here and not out there among the living you are just not that important anymore. After a while you know you are being forgotten and there isn't a thing in the world you can do about it. It's not a nice thing to accept but after a while you have to.

I knew that after a few months Cathy was back at school and didn't think of me half as much as she did at first, and when I first came to notice that it wasn't hard to see that any memory she had of me was fading away a little more each day. At first it really hurt my feelings and I was very angry at her for going on with her life as if I wasn't a part of it, but after a few weeks of being mad I came to understand that what she was doing was totally natural. She was going on with her life, which is what the living have to do if they're going to have any kind of happy life in the future.

It was even worse than that when Mommy and Daddy started not coming by so regularly. At first they'd be by almost every day. They'd come and I'd hear the car pull up and then they'd have something new to put on my grave, a birthday present, a Christmas tree on Christmas Eve, a pink bunny at Easter. Then they bought me a golden vase with colorful plastic flowers in it to sit in a stand by my marker, along with a windmill with chimes where the blades went around and musical notes jingled in the wind.

But after a while their visits became infrequent, and sometimes my vase and windmill would fall over if the wind blew hard and a storm came up.

Sometimes they would lay on the ground for a few days until Mommy or Daddy came by and put them back into place again.

Those were the times when I would get really sad.

But this is what made me smile.

For a while I'd taken notice of an old man who walked by on a regular basis. It took me a while to see that he wasn't here to visit anybody, but was just coming every day to walk. I could tell he didn't have a job to go to and was retired because he had gray hair and he didn't have a lot of spring in his step like young people do, but he would walk by going along as fast as he could, and sometimes he was quiet and I knew he was thinking and sometimes he would sing songs under his breath and even talk out loud to himself. He was just enjoying being alone out in the sunshine and the fresh air and getting a little closer every day to the end of his own life and making peace with himself about it.

I like to think that was what he was thinking about.

But he stopped one day when he saw my vase had toppled over. He picked it up and secured it back in the stand, bent over and tried tightening the screws with his finger. He set my windmill up and turned the blades to see if they would go around, then he listened to the sound of my chimes.

He smiled down at me.

"There you go, Melinda Joan," he said. "Everything's all right again. You don't have to worry. I'll keep an eye on you from now on."

He walked away and I watched him. I heard my chimes making music with the wind.

I don't know his name, but he comes by almost every day now. I wait for him to come. I look forward to seeing him. I like the sound of his voice. It helps, you know, for someone to know you're here. Nobody ever wants to be forgotten.

# HILLCREST ESTATES

## Edward Giles Parkhurst
## 1951-2007
## Gone But Not Forgotten

It came as a big surprise to me when I dropped dead on Christmas Day serving Communion at the church, especially since I didn't ever have any heart trouble in my life before then and I was feeling fine right up to the last minute. The only problem I had was I was getting more and more blind by the day, although I was still driving and working and trying to go along the same as usual. I had to make sure I was home before dark and to not go anywhere but work and church every day because I had the way to get to both those places memorized by then, but I still had to constantly be careful at whatever I was doing because if I didn't watch it I'd walk into a door or trip over something in the backroom at the store or run over a curb stanchion if I didn't know it was there, because the truth was I couldn't see it even if it was right in front of me if I was in a strange place. Only a few people knew how bad I was getting as far as seeing stuff went, and I didn't ever mention it much, on account I wanted to keep working until I could draw my full pension.

But I knew the layout of the church like the back of my hand, since I spent so much time there being a deacon and hanging out with Pastor and making sure everything got taken care of when it needed fixing or had to be replaced. I was kind of the fellow who looked in on everybody on their committees and made sure everything was going along smoothly and there wasn't some knucklehead gumming up the works, because you get a lot of that stuff these days, these men and women that want to come in and run everything and tell everybody how to do their jobs like they are the only ones who know what's shaking and everybody's supposed to come to them to get advice. Don't get me wrong—I love all my sisters and brothers at the church and want what's best for them whatever is going on, but sometimes you have to put your foot down and send some of these people on their way home so the job can get done right. I'm maybe not as up to the task as I used to be ten years ago, but I never let on how I couldn't see what was going on right beneath my eyes and just let them know I could see what was what even with my bad eyes. After all, old Ray Charles was blind as a bat but that never stopped him from writing songs and getting around, now did it? And nothing slowed me down either until that old aneurism or whatever it was came along and stopped me in my tracks on Christmas Day, 2007.

When I think about it and use the common sense God gave me, I don't feel too upset over getting called home at an early age. Maybe there were a few more things I would have liked to have done before I passed, like go on another ocean tour like the one Charlene and I went on back in 2002, when we cruised the Bahamas and all those islands out there in the Mediterranean. Of course, Charlene had to get off at every port and shop all day until her tongue was hanging out—I went with her some, but only a couple of times—because most of the time I stayed onboard and sampled out the free food and stayed up on deck on a lawn chair and looked at some of these women parading around in front of me. I was always looking at women, but I knew better than trying to touch them with improper intent on my mind. I settled for just giving them a hug at work or church and let that be it, just tell them I loved them and how faithful I was to them, all like a joke, you know. And anyway, when I think about it now, there ain't a bit of use getting all sad and depressed over not getting to go on another cruise, because as blind as I was getting before Jesus came and got me, I couldn't have seen much of anything on a cruise whatsoever, be it sightseeing or women passing by me.

Look at it this way. I was fifty-six when I keeled over, and the fact that it happened when it did was truly just a godsend and a blessing when you think about it. If I'd have not passed and stayed alive for the years to come I would have never been able to make it to retirement without getting declared disabled. I would have had to give up driving and watching TV (I used to watch TV all day long on the days I was off, when Charlene was gone to work and all the kids were gone to school or working or whatever, sit there in my recliner and eat cookies and drink coffee and watch "Tarzan" and "The Rifleman" and "Wanted Dead or Alive") and being a deacon and taking up the offering and serving communion and all those things I always did. I couldn't watch any sports on television at all or read the paper or nothing, and that would have really got to me after a while, so I guess it is God knows what He's doing and you don't need to question Him about what's right or wrong in your world.

Praise God!

I guess the thing I remember the most after that Christmas Day was my visitation on Wednesday and my funeral on Thursday. There were multitudes of people from the church that came by the auditorium, where they had me in my casket up in front of the dais where Pastor preached every Sunday, right in front of the communion table with the inscription "This Do in Remembrance of Me." If it had been left up to me I would have asked for folks to not send any flowers, because in real life they always made my nose itch and my eyes run, but Charlene, being the way she is, just let everybody infest the auditorium with arrangements and wreaths and bouquets of every plant and flower anybody is ever going to see, and when everything got delivered and they all got set up on their stands and such you couldn't hardly make me out up there in my casket except for a little opening where you could peek in and see me reposed there in my suit with my arms folded. No sir, I would have done things a lot different. I would have cleared out the place so people who suffered the same way I did might be able to breathe the tiniest bit.

But the visitation wasn't so bad other than being crowded with all the horticulture getting in the way. It was the funeral that played upon my mind so much. It was just over the top the way it went, and I guess being right there in the middle of it and having no choice about getting up and leaving made me get restless and start suffering in my head long before it got done.

Let me tell you about a black funeral if you've never been to one before. It would take a lot of explaining to my white-folk friends if I was trying to let them know what they're going to be in for in advance. Black folk already have a good idea what's fixing to happen when you go out the door for a ceremony sending somebody off to Heaven and Paradise and such, how once you close your door and lock it and get in your car to go to the church or the funeral home it's going to be a while before you make it back. You got to make sure you've turned off the stove and the lights are out and you've got somebody who's going to come by and let the dog out while you're away, because you're going to be gone for quite some time.

White people don't understand this. Most of them ain't ever been to a black funeral before because most of them only know black folks from working with them or going to school and maybe being on a team with them or having some black woman come by the house to clean or a black man to come by and cut the yard and such. It's kind of rare for white people to have blacks as friends and spend a lot of time with them, maybe even go to church together, because even if the century changed and Y-2K didn't kill us all things didn't change all that much from one year to the next. Whites still tended to stay away from blacks, and there was still that attitude that the blacks were going to erupt one day and come and kill everybody, and the blacks weren't a whole lot better because a lot of them thought that might be a pretty good idea. Even my big church couldn't keep everybody from having bad thoughts about white people, how they couldn't be trusted and were dangerous and all, thinking about the same way white folks thought about us. It wasn't as bad as it used to be, but it wasn't anywhere near good. Both sides just covered it up a little better than before.

I had a little of that attitude in me, but not much. See, I'd worked in a grocery store ever since I was sixteen, and I'd been around lots of white people over the course of forty years. I had this big personality, see, and I got along with everybody, and I'm not bragging when I say that they all clamored to get along with me. I was a popular guy even if I was blacker than the Ace of Spades. White people really and genuinely liked me, especially white women, and I could have had a lot of white girlfriends over the years if I'd wanted to.

But I didn't. I knew better.

When I died I had two really good white friends, Jimmy and Daniel, Jimmy who I called Fats because of his beer belly and Daniel who I called Wiz, because he was about as smart as anybody I ever met working, seeing how he could do books and work with numbers and everything. The way it was then was Fats and Wiz and I were the smartest people in the store, so smart we kept to ourselves most of the time and stayed away from the knuckleheads we worked with, who generally didn't have a lick of sense if you watched them for any amount of time at all. Me and Fats would work together on the grocery side, stocking shelves and building displays and such, Fats as the head clerk and me as the backup, while Wiz was up in the office doing books and running the front end even though he wasn't officially head of it—he was too smart for that, knowing all along that if he was the head of what went on up there he'd get blamed for everything wrong when it came to customer service or money missing. Just like us, he had his bases covered. Management treated the three of us really good because we knew what we were doing and didn't need anybody riding our backs trying to get us to work like they had to do with the rest of the people. They left us alone and knew better than to bother us.

Oh, we'd get new managers in sometimes, heads and assistants, and at first they'd come in and try and tell us how to do things and try and change our schedules and such, but after a while they'd realize they'd done nothing but cut their own throats and then decide to do like everybody before and leave us alone.

The three of us worked fifteen years together like that. We'd work the same schedule on the same days and take the same days off, and then we'd go to ball games together at night. I'd drive so Fats and Wiz could drink all the beer they wanted and not worry about it, because I don't think I had but one swallow of beer and a half a glass of wine my whole life. I didn't need any of that stuff to enjoy myself. I was happy already.

But to make a long story short, when I dropped dead Charlene had to pick out who my pallbearers were going to be, and so she chose Fats and Wiz because we were all such good friends for so long, so that's how I ended up with two crackers sitting on the front row where they could look through all the ferns and flowers and greenery and see me lying there.

Actually, I thought it was pretty funny, especially when I thought about how Fats and I used to have these fake arguments with each other all the time, calling each other names and acting like we were fixing to have a fight in front of folks so it would freak them out if they didn't know better. I used to tell Fats to shut his mouth before I popped him, call him a racist and to go back to his Klan meeting, and he'd call me a cricket and a spearchucker and stuff like that, and like I say, if people didn't know what was going on and weren't used to it, they'd start getting really uncomfortable and start looking for some reason to leave, which is what we wanted to begin with. We liked getting rid of those idiots quick as we could. And Wiz would always get in the middle of it, acting like he was trying to break up the fight and keep us from killing each other.

So there was Fats and Wiz, my two thoroughly-honky friends, sitting there on the front row for my funeral with no possible way to escape. I couldn't help but think of it as the best practical joke I had ever played on them.

See, we were always messing with each other when we weren't busy messing with everybody else. That dern Fats would load up a trash bag full of all his empty Budweiser cans, and when he got one good and full he'd drive it over to my house and dump it in the yard. One time he came during a rainstorm and drove his truck up in the yard and made ruts in the wet lawn and tore up the mud driving around, and he'd ask me from time to time if I needed him to come over and do some plowing. I'd get him back, though. I'd always pick me out the ugliest female employee there was at the store and tell her how Fats had a crush on her but was just too shy to say anything. I don't know how many times he had ugly women following him around smiling at him. And Fats and I didn't leave Wiz out of the fun either. We told everybody who'd listen how we were pretty sure he might be the Unabomber.

The service went on and on with people testifying and solos and duets and full-choir gospel songs getting sung, hands clapping and pastor preaching and prayers getting offered up that lasted ten minutes or so at a time. Pretty soon we'd been going at it almost three hours, and I could see Wiz and Fats glancing at their watches and kind of looking at each other from time to time, and I knew they were ready for this to get done, and it tickled me a great bit because I knew they hadn't seen nothing yet.

The service started at ten, and it was coming up on three when it came time to wheel me out of the church and load me up in the hearse. I noticed how Fats and Wiz got in Wiz's Toyota and followed us along in the procession. I guess they thought if they came together they could take off as soon as the burial was over and not have to wait around anymore. There was a part of me that wanted to get in the back seat with them and tell them how they had another think coming.

The burial service lasted another hour or so. This was after we drove for about forty-five minutes out of town to say goodbye to my childhood home and then doubled back through rush-hour traffic to get to Summer Haven. I'll give them credit for one thing, though. They didn't take off when the first shovelful of dirt landed on my coffin; they stuck around until the diggers got through. Then they came up and said goodbye to Charlene, which I appreciated, especially when I knew they were dying to leave the entire time. The funny thing was they had a basketball game they were going to that night, and they'd have to hightail it across town to get there for tipoff.

They tore out of there finally, but I didn't let it bother me. They'd just got through spending the whole day learning how black folks handle death. Not too many white people would have lasted through it, but they did, so I gave them credit.

They were and still are my friends.

Mine eyes have already seen the glory, let me tell you. I've been to my heaven and found my peace and I'm free now. I can go wherever I want whenever I want, and there's lots of places I call Paradise. It's nice to be able to go to them at the beat of my heavenly heart.

And one of those places is here. It's nice to find myself here on earth sometimes, here in this place where now and then Fats and Wiz come by to visit. One of these days I might just holler out at them and scare their honky butts to death, just to get a laugh.

# PEACEFUL ACRES

## Geneva Ann Blanton
## (1897-1973)
## His Eye is On the Sparrow

**A**in't but one person that comes by anymore and he ain't family at all. Guess I should be glad for that much, since there ain't many of my kin left in the world. There's two granddaughters and two grandsons that are still around, but it's been a long time since any of them's come around. The granddaughters are married and moved out of the state long ago after their mother, my daughter, and her husband both died, and one of the grandsons is dying of cancer last I knew and the other wouldn't come by to pay his respects if you paid him, on account he never liked me when I was living, and the truth is I can't really blame him. I was sort of a grouchy old woman back when he was little, having lost Wallace in 1947 when he drowned on a fishing trip, leaving me with five children to look after. Thank the Lord three of them were out of the house by then, but I still had Tommy and Wilma to worry about. I had to take in renters for the upstairs ever since then, which was the only way I was going to get by, because I sure as shooting didn't want to give up my house and go live with any of my children. I'd have never been comfortable doing that.

Yes, when that Joseph was little he and I didn't much get along at all. He'd come over here with his momma and daddy and big sister and I could tell just by the look in his eye that he was soon going to be into something, I could see the way he was, and so I knew I'd have to put a stop to it before it ever got started, because it was for derned tooting his mother and my son Billy weren't going to do it. Billy was just too quiet and Edith was too flighty worrying about how her hair looked and if her shoes matched her out-fit. They'd let those kids go unsupervised too much, in my opinion. Elaine wasn't too bad, I reckon, since she was a girl and the oldest and had a little bit of sense in her, but that boy Joseph I knew was going to be trouble unless somebody got a handle on him, and the more I saw of him the more I knew it was going to have to be me to be the one who'd have to reign him in.

Well, the long and the short of it is it's slow and lonesome around here at Summer Haven sometimes. It's a good thing I don't have to stay here all the time, because that could get tedious, the waiting and the thinking and all, but luckily I'm at a point where I can come and go as I please. Wallace was never one to hang around a place after he was done with it, so he's gone straightaway to the Hereafter and not come back like some of us do, those of us who can't quite let it go yet because we're looking for some way to make whatever we were doing that went unfinished turn out to our sat-isfaction. I can't say I have a whole slew of things I want to get resolved, but I do know there's a few things I'd like to see the finish of before I'm gone forever.

I still get flowers on my grave from time to time, but they sure don't come from anybody in the family. What it is, I'm pretty sure, is this fellow who was a friend of one of my other grandsons, Allen, who's passed now too and is buried with my oldest son and daughter-in-law about thirty yards down from me. That grandson, Paul, died at age fifty-nine, AIDs I think it was, and this man who I'm certain was his partner back in real life comes around now and then to put flowers on his grave, and I've seen him walk up this way with artificial flowers in a vase and put them on my oldest daughter's grave, which is at my feet, and then on mine and Wal-lace's. I guess that's saying something nice about the man, even if I think he and Allen were homosexuals and sweet on each other and are probably both going to end up in hell together. But I'm not so convinced about things like that as I used to be. I have to admit it's a good thing to do to remember his friend and not only garnish his gravesite but have the decency to take care of the relatives buried around him too.

And he's not even a real member of the family either.

I do sometimes wonder what that grandson of mine is up to these days. By my count he has to be sixty-six by now. I wonder if he's retired from working and if he's raised a family along the way. My goodness but the time has gone by so much it's hard to imagine him like that, with a wife and kids who've already grown up and gone their way and probably don't know the first thing about me. I wouldn't expect them to, because that would require my grandson to tell them something about my life or where I was buried or something like that, and I know for certain he has never done anything like that.

Of course, I don't guess I blame him. I'm the one who brought this on myself by being so strict with him and making sure he behaved when he was at my house. I think of it now and I wonder how important that all was back then. But that was the way I was. I thought everybody ought to behave the same way I did or they'd die and go to Hell for sure. I still don't think I was too far wrong. I haven't, as yet, learned exactly where Hell is—I haven't been shown the light on things like that so far—but I can at least say I don't think a lot of these people who did not follow the Lord and his Rules and Regulations while they were alive are not up in Heaven before me. You just can't tell me that. Perhaps I haven't been granted complete access to the Pearly Gates just yet but I think that's one of those things everybody has to go through before they get there. I don't know anywhere in the Bible where God's Holy Word says how long everyone's judgement is supposed to last. It doesn't say whether you get told yes or no right off the bat or if the Lord takes His time and looks at your works and your ways your entire life since you were saved and decides over some period of time whether you are going in and when that will be or if you need to wait and do a little penance or if there's some more judgement to come that's going to decide whether you endure the fires of Hell or not.

I don't know how it is I know these things, but they come to me sometimes just out of the blue and I know they're true. I know for a fact that although my long-lost grandson Joseph may not ever come around here to pay his respects to me or Wallace he still thinks about us from time to time. I find that a little funny since he never even knew Wallace in the first place, because like I mentioned Wallace drowned three years before Joseph was even born, so I suppose the boy wonders sometimes what his grandfather was like and all that. I bet he wonders if Wallace was as strict as me, and if he might have liked Wallace had he not drowned. I don't know about that. Wallace wasn't exactly a bundle of joy all the time. He kept quiet and never had a lot to say, preferring to stay in his shop six days a week and go off fishing on Sundays when he should have been in church. We argued about him not attending services a lot back then, but Wallace was more determined to be in his boat than to be sitting by me in a pew.

My senses tell me, though I don't know how, that at some point that boy Joseph bought into one of those trace your ancestors programs and did him some research on me and Wallace and his other grandparents and all his aunts and uncles. I don't know what or how much he found out, but it must have satisfied him, because he never came by here to study our tombstones or inquire about us at the funeral home office or anything like that. I guess he just wanted to know if he was white or if he had some colored ancestors or if we'd been die-hard Confederates during the Civil War or something. A lot of these people living around here nowadays get offended and ashamed if they find out one of their relatives owned slaves or shot an Indian once, like they wish to be above such things and act like their family was always high and mighty and holy, but I suspect it's just a lot of poking around to make sure there wasn't something hiding in the family tree that was going to jump out and embarrass them later on. I don't understand what the big problem is. History is history, and there's nothing you can do to change it.

Now what does really bother me is that there's this big old hawk that flies around out here that's taken to sitting on my tombstone just about every single day and looking around to see if there's something moving he can go snatch up. Or maybe he's just tired of flying around and hunting and needs to take a break and this is where he's chosen to sit—I don't know. All I can tell you is it gets on my nerves, him sitting there like that. It's not that he's really doing something bad or anything, but I know he's sitting there thinking about something and I don't know what it is, and after a while I want to tell him to stop, to go somewhere else, because it disturbs me to not know what is going on in somebody's mind, whether it's a hawk or a little boy or who it is.

In real life I always liked to be on top of things, to know what was going on and offer my wisdom on how to go about getting all the problems solved and everybody towing the line. I was that way with Wallace and my children, and I made them know that was the way it was going to be.

But you come across something like this hawk or that boy Joseph, who just don't care and don't listen to what somebody like me has to tell them, and even though I'm in this place waiting it still worries me to no end how to change this. I just hope before God finally calls me home I'll find the answer.

# GREEN PASTURES

## DAVID CALVIN HOPKINS
## (1947-2016)
## ALWAYS IN OUR HEARTS

Yeah, that's my name on the stone sitting here beside Momma and Daddy, but that was all my brother's doing for their sake and because that's the way they wanted it in their will, to have me buried there beside them. Well, I want to tell you that my name being etched on a stone here is just for show to anybody who wants to come by and visit, because I'm not buried here or anywhere in any goddamn casket with my body pumped full of formaldehyde and methanol and all that crap they do to you when they've got you on the table, because I just wasn't going to goddamn stand for it. I told everybody who'd listen what to do with me, and for the most part when I kicked off they got it done.

Maybe it was colon cancer or maybe it was just a heart attack that did the trick, but all I know is I was okay one week and the next thing you know I was gone. But at least I didn't suffer all that much. They told me about the colon cancer and how it was going to be touch and go treating it, so I lived with pills for a year instead of radiation, but they kept telling me I was going to have to get it done eventually. I kept putting them off, though, because I may be a dumbass in a lot of ways but I'm not stupid and I've always known which way the wind was blowing when it came to crap coming down. I knew already I was on borrowed time and I might as well try and get everything in under the wire before the fucking Grim Reaper came to get me. It could be I thought so much about it and worried so much that it put stress on me I didn't know was happening, and so the old ticker just called it quits while I was sleeping. I'm not really bitching about the whole process, because at least it didn't take forever to happen and I didn't dry up and become a living skeleton in front of everybody. Hell, my old dog even died about three weeks before me, so I didn't have to worry about what was going to happen to him when I was gone.

They hauled me off and took me down the road to this cheap-ass cremation joint that I'd gone and fixed everything up with about a month before. All they did was charge me a straight fee and a small transportation payment to the place and I was good to go. Janice came and picked up my ashes in a cardboard container and brought me home and set me on the living room table. I guess she didn't know what to do with me really, even though I'd told her a bunch of times how I wanted to get sprinkled into the Atlantic Ocean. All she had to do was go down to the pier and empty me over the side and that would do it, but she let me sit there three days before she and my buddy Warren and his wife Sharon finally smoked a joint in the living room and then went down to the pier in Warren's Bronco and dropped me in while the sun was setting. Nobody cried or anything like that, probably because they were too stoned to know what they were doing, but it could have been because this was about the best way any of this shit could happen and they were glad it was all over with.

I was glad too. I didn't even have a funeral, which was fine with me. Fuck that bullshit.

Janice wasn't ever much at being organized or getting stuff done properly, so she never did get around to phoning my brother and telling him I'd died until the day I started swimming with the fishes, so he wasn't present to see me get sprinkled or use his expertise to get me an obituary in the paper or a proper funeral or anything. When he found out I was already a member of the Atlantic Ocean roster he decided there wasn't much of a use to come down and try to settle any of my effects, since having talked to Janice a couple of times on the phone he'd come to the conclusion she was crazy as Great Grannie's bedbug and best avoided if there was no huge reason to be in her vicinity, so he stayed back in Murfreesboro and contacted the funeral home in Athens and drove down and purchased a stone out of what was left over from Momma and Daddy's estate. That's how fucking organized he was. They'd both been dead over ten years and he still had what assets they had left from the estate gathered together in a separate account so it wouldn't get mixed up with his. I guess that's why he was the executor instead of me, since he was the son who was dependable and honest and didn't ever spend time in jail for breaking and entering or assault and battery or possession or any of that shit I got myself into. In my old age my last few years I got to where occasionally I'd be ashamed of myself for the hell I put my folks through, but I have to admit most times I didn't think about it at all. Come to think about it, there wasn't too much I did think about for a long time, other than playing my guitar and driving a fast car and having a dog around to live with me. I had women come and go and even married three of them, but sooner or later they'd be gone and I'd be in-between, but I always had a dog.

I started out with this collie I had named Lady who an old man gave me when I was in high school because she was nervous and skittish and kept wanting to bite and snap at anybody and everybody, but after I had her a week or two she was all right with me, which wasn't surprising, because back then and all through my life I always had a way with dogs. Too bad that didn't translate to human beings, who as a whole always drove me to the point where I'd snap and bite at them or come up the side of their head before long, which was something that always got me in some kind of trouble. I guess that sort of shit had a lot to do with helping me to get locked up a few times. I was anti-social and out of control a lot.

Anyway, Lady ended up getting hit by a car when I let her outside one night, and after that I had a German Shepherd named Rex and an Afghan I named Buddini after Muhammed Ali's trainer. I didn't have very good luck with any of my dogs for a while because either something would happen to them, they'd get poisoned or hit by cars or I'd get locked up or have to go into rehab and have to give them away, but I always had to get another one whenever I re-entered the real world afterward because the one thing that was for sure was I couldn't live without a dog. I couldn't tell you how many dogs I had while I was alive.

I couldn't live without a guitar either. Back when I was doing some serious drugs I broke into a house and stole a pile of money from a desk drawer and went to a pawn shop and bought a Les Paul Epiphone electric guitar, and I'm not shitting you when I say I got pretty damn good on it. I'd played guitar maybe five years before I got hold of the Les Paul, from the time I was thirteen or so, and by the time I was in high school I was good enough to be playing with bands around town and after a time even formed my own group with a couple of my friends, Danny who played bass and Ronnie who played drums. We were pretty good and started playing around town and taking gigs, and that's where I picked up my liking for drugs. I liked taking them and then got to selling them, and I lived the high, fast life for a good while.

I got busted eventually, naturally, and I spent time in diversionary programs and a few stints in the workhouse and in and out of rehab clinics, all of which Momma and Daddy paid for. I was grateful—don't get me wrong—and I always promised to do better from then on, but the sad part of it is it never lasted.

I was just a wild man. I was just a fuckup. I would always find myself back on the same road to Worthlessness time and time again. Maybe it was I didn't have any willpower or maybe I just couldn't ever bring myself to tell myself no, but whatever the reason was I'd soon find myself back down in the quicksand again.

The truth of it is I can't blame it on me not having brains enough to do any better with my life, because they gave us these intelligence tests back in high school and I scored way off the top of the chart on them. I kept having counselors and teachers tell me I was a genius and all I needed to do was apply myself, but they couldn't see that there was something in me that made it impossible to do such a thing. I'm not trying to make excuses for myself, but I'm not bullshitting when I say there were warring factions in me that made me do strange things to make the voices in my head shut the hell up.

I was damn good on the guitar, but I got into coke and heroin and shit so bad I had to sell my Epiphone, and then the only way I had dough to live on and buy more drugs was to take to stealing and breaking in homes and dealing myself. I knew I'd get caught one way or another someday but by then I didn't care.

I remember back when I was in high school—I can't remember if I was in tenth or eleventh grade—the state was building a bridge over the Hiwassee River to connect Athens and Sweetwater on the other side, and two of my buddies and me had parked my 56 Chevy up by the side of the bridge after the workers had left for the day. We smoked a joint and looked down at the river which was probably thirty yards down and maybe more, and when we were good and buzzed I made a bet with them I'd take a dive off for twenty bucks apiece. They took me up on it because they didn't really think I was crazy enough to do it.

Well, I for damned sure was. I jumped. I stood right in the middle of the bridge on a concrete rail and dove off before I could talk myself out of it. I was a big, strong guy, and nothing had hurt me so far in life, so I didn't think this would either.

It did, though. I threw my back out of whack for what turned out to be the rest of my life, and I was never the same again. I had to take pain pills because there wasn't any surgery that was going to fix me, and I took so damn many that my problems with narcotics and drugs moved along into high gear.

I wasn't ever an invalid, though. I learned to keep going no matter what, and sometimes I lived pretty high on the hog and sometimes I was broke without a place to stay or a penny in my pocket; either way, I couldn't ever seem to settle down and stay in one job and live in one place. I was always on the move, always looking to find a place where I'd never have to worry or work ever again. You'd think with my high freaking I.Q. I'd have found out a whole lot faster that there is no such place—at least not for somebody like me, who could never spot a good deal when he saw it, who always believed there was something better that was going to come about once I cruised down the interstate and found the right exit ramp.

Hell, I do all this talking and tell all these stories, and every time it sounds like I'm blaming somebody else for a life that went under and sideways more often than it stayed on the straight and narrow. Not true. Me, I'm my worst enemy. Always have been, and I hang around out here knowing it's all over and there's nothing I or anybody else can do about it, and it seems like I'm crying about it but I'm not. I'm to blame and I know it. It's not my three ex-wives or my brother or anybody who I thought had it out for me that did this. It was all me.

I confess—okay? I'm an asshole. It's all out there now for me and everybody else to see, so maybe by owning up to it I can rest easy from here on out. Do you think? I'd like for it to be as easy as that but I'm pretty doubtful. I don't know if there's such a thing as resting in peace for me. If there is I sure as shit haven't seen it yet.

# PARADISE VISTA

## JEFFREY DEAN CHURCHWELL
## (1950-2016)

## MAKE A JOYFUL NOISE UNTO THE LORD

**I**'m more than convinced that a lot of people I used to know from high school and college are sure I died from complications of AIDs, since it was such a royal affair when I came out of the closet when I got away from home attending the University of North Carolina. I guess I was far enough away by then that when reports started coming down on my sexual preferences they took on some sort of mythical state, like I was the only person in the state of Tennessee who's ever come out gay.

But I suppose it was a little bit of a surprise, since from all appearances for so many years everyone seemed to assume that I was a big ladies' man. I went out on dates and went to the proms and when there was a party you could bet that girls would be lining up just to pair off with me. That just goes to show you how much people know about anything. Everybody thinks they're these big experts and pigeonhole others into little categories and think they're on top of everything. I guess it really flipped a lot of them out when they found out I wasn't a red-blooded American boy like they thought I was all along.

I even fooled myself, if you want to know the truth. For a long time I didn't know what it was I was feeling inside me. I couldn't have told you I was gay or not even under sworn oath, because I was so mixed up about it. There I was, with girls begging me to ask them out, and I couldn't understand why I wasn't the least excited about it. I even made myself try to be straight and fake it, like I had something to be ashamed about and it was me who needed to make some sort of major adjustment. See, it was different in those days. If somebody was found to be queer they were either teased and shamed and jeered at or else somebody had to take it upon himself to beat the shit out of that person because he was an enemy to mankind. At least by waiting until I went away to school and got around others with the same inclinations as me I didn't have to wear a scarlet Q around my neck and get beaten senseless every time I turned around, which in my secret heart was about the only thing I felt like I accomplished during those turbulent years of secondary school.

What I did, and I guess it seemed pretty strange to everyone, I don't know, was I just went away from home to college and I never came back, not for the summer, not for Christmas or Thanksgivings or birthdays or anything. It was like I was dead and everyone had missed the funeral. I just vanished off the face of the earth, and I didn't take phone calls or answer letters or anything. See, in my day and time there weren't such things as Facebook or email or long distance phone calls you didn't have to pay through the nose for, so by being about a million miles away I didn't have to worry about being in contact too much with my old life, and I believed I was safe to start up a new life and never have to worry about what anybody said or thought ever again.

From that point on in my life, I never tried to stay in the closet or hide my sexual preferences from anyone, but I don't think I could have kept it that much more of a secret even if I tried. When I went to classes or went to any on-campus events, it was like girls still tried to catch my eye and talk to me, like I was some prime candidate for romance. I suppose I could have saved them a lot of trouble by letting them know my orientation, but the truth of it is I enjoyed the attention coming my way. I was also in those days— and still was until the day I drew my last breath—sort of a trickster and a social scientist. I liked playing people along. I didn't do any-thing mean or underhanded in my actions, but it was fun to flirt with girls and watch their eyes twinkle, all the time knowing that if I'd been of another bent I could have any of them with the wave of a hand, and such a feeling made me feel special in some strange way I can't describe. After I graduated, it was the same way in the office I worked in. I took a job in computer programming in the admissions department at school and was around on campus the next thirty years of my life, working after a time as the head of the department and being falsely known as a mysterious eligible bachelor. Of course, I never went out on dates with any of these girls, but I liked giving them a thrill and setting their silly hearts aflutter by going to after-game parties and dances and concerts, and later attending post-work meetings for drinks and laughs on Fridays and watching their tactics as they attempted coming on with me. That was where the social scientist part came into play. I enjoyed seeing the behavior of those around me, the women as they tried to figure out how to seduce me, the tiny strands of jealousy from the men around who were simply dying to be held in such regard by all the women as I was, and those persons on the fringe who watched all the interplay and tried to come to some understanding of exactly where I was coming from, what it was that made me tick and seemed to cause me to be more special than anyone else in the vicinity.

In the meantime, I was able to have relationships with other men in both long and short durations. I was smart enough not to broadcast my every move publicly, but I discovered there were lots of places two men could go and not stand out like a sore thumb to the rest of the world. All I had to do was get in my car and drive off-campus a ways and all would be well. I could eat dinner or go to the movies and no one would bat an eye, probably because I didn't make a big deal out of such things and I refused to have anything to do with men who acted garish or broadcasted their sexuality for the watching world just to get noticed and draw attention. No, my life and my feelings were a sacred, private thing to me, and I never felt the need to argue my case or garner praise for my courage or any of that rigmarole. As far as I was concerned, the world was free to do what they wanted and I was too. We could both go down the paths we chose and everyone could be happy and content at the same time.

Through all this smooth existence, I never truly had very deep feelings for anyone I was involved with for too long a time. I suppose it was I had been playing my solitaire detached life for such a long time that when it did occur to me that I was getting a little long in the tooth and was still out on the fringes playing the dating game in a subdued and quiet way that it first came to my attention that if I didn't watch it I might be in danger of being one of those stereotypical lonely old homosexuals in my old age, and I pictured in my mind people seeing me pass by and clucking their tongues and saying how they'd known what I'd been up to all my life and how it was just too bad that a person with as much personality and wit as me could wind up having nowhere to go and no one to be around in their golden years. I didn't really think it would ever be that way, but I knew after all my years of analysis the way people tended to think, and I didn't like the fact that perhaps all the people I'd charmed for so many years would one day be talking behind my back and feeling sorry for me in some kind of a superior mindset.

Luckily, all that changed almost instantaneously. Maybe it was because I changed my usual manner and opened myself up to the world a little more than before, but it turned out I met the Tennis coach from the Athletic Department at an alumni lunch, and it was sort of an aborted version of "Some Enchanted Evening" from South Pacific in a way, since it was daytime and not evening and he wasn't across a crowded room at all but sitting across from me at one of the tables, and he looked very handsome with his premature gray hair and his sport coat sans tie and his very neat goatee, and we talked about the way college students of today behaved and how it used to be back in the days when we were in school, and it turned out he had been two years ahead of me here at school and we'd somehow never met, but now that we had it seemed like a good idea for us to go play tennis together on the coming Saturday morning. He could get us a court with no problem. He had a set of keys. And if anyone was already there, he could tell them to get lost. He was in charge.

Andrew and I stayed together for twelve years. We bought

a nice older house in the quiet section of town and never acknowledged in any way our lifestyle from any point in the spectrum. I suspect people had their ideas and suspicions about us, but we never made anything known as to whether we were gay or not. Andrew was just like me in that way. He simply didn't think what he did in our leisure hours was anybody's business, so he never bothered explaining it or saying yes or no to any of their unspoken questions. We spent our time dining out or cooking at home (I don't know which one of us was the better cook—I'd say it was a tossup) and when we went out it was to a movie or a play or perhaps a concert if there was anyone we wanted to hear. Mostly we stayed in, reading and watching movies on the cable, and once a year during the summers we would always take a long trip to somewhere, on a cruise or flying off to another country or renting a luxury SUV and driving from one end of the country to another just to explore and sightsee. We had a wonderful, private life together.

But just a few months before his retirement Andrew and his tennis team went on a Friday and Saturday trip to the conference tournament in Durham, and on the way there the driver had a stroke while driving and the bus went off the road, killing the driver and three of the passengers and injuring eight more. Andrew was killed immediately, and it took me a long time to come to grips with it. I don't think I ever accepted his death one hundred percent, but that probably stemmed from my way of thinking that if I didn't buy into the fact totally that he was gone then it was like it hadn't happened. I could pretend Andrew was just on a trip and that when I came home in the afternoon he would be home again.

I went on like that for about a year.

Finally, I had to re-surface and start breathing real human air again, so I went back to work on a parttime basis and tried to get into a routine. I was fairly happy but never could quite get on board with my old existence, probably because there were too many reminders of Andrew connected to it. I always found myself anticipating seeing him when it came close to quitting time each day, and because that wasn't true I couldn't help but get down over it. I knew I was going to have to have a complete change of scenery if I was ever going to get back in the groove again.

That's when a friend from my old office called me and asked if I'd like to come work with her at a tour service. Because of my great people skills, she told me, and because I knew how to communicate and make people feel comfortable I would be perfect as a tour guide for some of the Civil War sites and historical homes in the area. The money was great and the hours were flexible—I could pretty much work whenever I wanted to—and before long I'd given my notice and was riding along on a charter bus with this fellow named Conrad who looked like Raymond Burr, and Conrad and I would ride around groups of thirty or so and show them where the Confederates won a battle but ended up losing the War, along with mansions and plantations and old schoolhouses where kiddos learned to cipher and recite their ABCs. I'd work three days a week and draw more money than I ever had in my legitimate business career, and on top of that the tips were incredible.

It got to a point, though, where I didn't feel so peppy most days, and after a couple of months of feeling rundown I visited my doctor. I knew there was something wrong somewhere between the pain in my joints and the way I was losing weight and coughing a lot. I wasn't wrong. It took a couple of weeks and all sorts of tests but the verdict was lymphoma, and the bad part was that it had already spread to my lymph nodes and beyond. For the next year and a half I had radiation treatments and chemotherapy and bone marrow procedures to go along with a regiment of pills and potions, but nothing could stop it.

I began wasting away, shriveling up and beginning to look like an Egyptian mummy, and I found myself staying in and waiting for the end, which I prayed to come quickly and get me out of the life I had remaining. About the only time I left the house was to amble through a grocery store or go place flowers on Andrew's gravesite, which is in another cemetery in his family's plot, and other than go back to the doctor every week or so and get told to keep fighting there was nothing to do but watch more movies and wait.

That last night I was watching A Star is Born with James Mason and Judy Garland—Andrew and I always loved that movie for some reason—and it came to the part where Norman Maine decided to walk out to the sea and end it all. I looked at the waves and the rising sun on the horizon and I felt myself going with him, like the water was rising up to my chest and it wouldn't be long at all.

And that was it. I was gone. I didn't even make it to the closing credits.

Per my wishes, I was buried back in Athens so what little of my family that was left would be able to visit me, but my heart was still in North Carolina, for it had been my home for so long. It is where I lived my life. The good thing is in my state of not being among the living anymore I can keep doing what I want and can will myself to stay in Chapel Hill forever. I don't regret such a decision. In a way I guess I'm pleasing everyone, being in both places for all time. Just like everything else I did in my life, I believe I've made the right choice.

# MOUNT HOPE

## STEPHEN LEE FRANKLIN
## (1951-1979)

## I'LL FLY AWAY

I wonder sometimes how many songs I wrote when I was coming up, when I was in my teens and just hanging out on the fringes in high school, or later when I got out in the real world and going into the army and heading off to Viet Nam. Nothing stopped me from writing songs at any time, not even when I was wading through marshes with a pack on my back wondering if in the next minute some Viet Cong was going to shoot me and I'd be dead before I knew it was coming. No, the whole time I was writing a song even while that was going on, up there in my head, and that's pretty much the way it was my entire life. No matter what kind of situation I was in, there was a song being composed in my brain, usually at the same time. It used to drive people who didn't know me crazy. They thought I was spastic or anal-retentive or something, but the folks who knew me, my family and friends, were used to it. They knew I was weird, but they didn't think anything bad was going to come from it. They just figured that was the way I was.

I don't think there was any big artistic leaning going on when I first got started. I was a freshman in high school and I saved up my money from cutting yards the entire summer and went down and found a cheap guitar at a salvage store in downtown Athens and bought it for twenty bucks, which was a fair amount of money in 1966. I wasn't so much into writing a good song as I was learning to play that guitar so girls would notice me. Turned out I got one out of two. I learned how to play all right, but the girls didn't give a shit about me one way or another. I told myself at least I didn't get shut out.

The good thing about learning how to play music was I discovered I could turn my attention to not only learning songs from other people but maybe writing a few of them myself, which is what I set out to do like a big wave of gangbusters. I didn't know the first thing about composing music at all in a formal way, couldn't read the notes on a page or anything like that, but I got to where I wasn't bad fumbling around on the frets and coming up with tunes by myself, and once I got the melody memorized in my head and could go to it anytime on the guitar, that's when it got fairly easy for the words to come along to go with it. I could have a tune going on with the guitar and pretty soon a couple of verses would start popping into my head.

Now, I'm not saying these early songs were masterpieces or anything like that, because they weren't. I was fourteen and fifteen and all I knew I either borrowed off of somebody on the radio or made it up myself, which I knew at that time that it wasn't any good. But I never gave up. You sure as hell can't fault me for that. I kept trying.

I got me a job at a Cee Bee grocery store when I turned sixteen, and after working my hind end off all that summer I was able to buy me an old Chevy pickup truck that looked like shit but still ran pretty fair, and so I was able to get around a little when I wasn't working or going to school and show up at talent shows and backyard parties and play anytime I got a chance. I never made no money or won a prize except for once, when I placed third in the school talent show and won ten dollars and a trophy. It didn't seem like much to anybody else but it meant something to me. I went downtown and bought a new used guitar and then filled that trophy with some of my daddy's whiskey and drank it down. I was a junior in high school with a new guitar and a bellyful of Old Charter. I was doing all right.

Course, it didn't help the cause none when I spent so much time playing parties and riding around having a big time that I ended up basically flunking out of high school, like that's actually possible and an easy thing to do or something. What happened is I just got so far behind it looked to me like I'd never be able to catch up, so instead of going back and knuckling down I just stopped going to school at all, which at the time wasn't really the smartest thing to do. But I did it anyway.

I knew the draft board was going to be calling my name but I tried to put it out of my mind for a time. I thought if I ignored it long enough it would go away, but after a while I knew that wasn't going to happen. I knew where my ass was headed, so I asked around and had several people tell me I'd do better if I'd just enlist on my own. I didn't have any discernable talents other than playing the guitar and writing songs, but I thought maybe they'd take pity on me because I'd screwed up and made a few bad decisions and put me somewhere where I could load trucks nine to five or mow some general's lawn and empty his trash five or six days a week. Heck, anything sounded acceptable to me as long as I wasn't getting shot at.

Well, none of that happened, just like I always knew in the pit of me it wasn't going to, and it wasn't long before I was down in Texas sweating in the sun learning how to put a rifle together and crawl on my belly like a rattlesnake. I burrowed under barbed wire fences and dug foxholes with the best of them, got my head buzzed and practiced running around with a full pack on my back all day. After they figured out I might be educated enough in the ways of the military I got transported to a waiting camp in Hoboken, New Jersey, where I'd never been in my life. While we were there I learned that was where Frank Sinatra was born, but I never got a chance to sight-see. Within two weeks I was on my way for a one-year tour of duty in Viet Nam.

I thought when I was first on my way to Nam that it was going to really freak me out and be life-changing for my future forever and ever, but it really didn't work out that way. I don't know if I've really been blessed by the Lord above in too many things in my life—I never was smart, I was pretty goddamned homely, I didn't come from a rich family, etc., etc., etc., but one thing I did have in my hip pocket was this uncanny ability to let things roll off my back like water off of a duck and not only get over something fast but pretty damn much forget it ever happened. That was the way it went with me and my Southeast Asia experience. It was awful and mind-blowing and death was always there tapping you on the shoulder all the time, but for me it simply turned into a procession of days, like somebody was shuffling a deck of cards and they were all going by so fast you couldn't read the face cards or the suits or tell anything about them, but in the case of me being in Viet Nam and hiking around all day with a rifle waiting for death to come and get me, this fast shuffle shit was exactly what I needed to get by. It was like everything that happened to me or was laid out in front of me got caught in this shuffle and before I knew it was over and done and long gone and couldn't be remembered or dwelled on because there was always something new coming along to take its place.

So I didn't live in fear or have bad dreams or spend time worrying about what might have become of me just an hour back, because all that was over now and I had to concentrate on whatever horrible or terrible thing was coming up next. And if it so happened nothing bad was to happen, I somehow knew better than to start rejoicing and feeling happy over it too much, because I knew the shuffle was going and something else was coming along toward me in a blur.

About the time my year deployment was coming to an end was when the country started deescalating and was doing all it could to get out of Nam without a lot of egg on its face, so I came home and stayed in a barrack in Wilmington, North Carolina for six months and that was it. I got discharged and was free to get back to my life.

The only problem with that is I really didn't have much of a life to get back to, since I didn't have any skills to speak of and there wasn't a college around that was going to admit me on the basis of my past transcripts, which were nothing but failures and incompletes. My dad was in a home for alcoholics and my mother had moved back to Oklahoma to live with her sister, and I didn't want nothing to do with trying to find her and showing up where I wasn't really wanted. See, I'd sort of worn out my welcome with my parents and pretty much the entire family with the way I was acting those couple of years before getting drafted. I was like the black sheep with everybody, and I didn't have any friends on top of that. But what else was new?

I took what money I had coming and bought an old Chevy 2 from a used car lot. I looked around town for a few days and didn't find anything worth renting or no place that was going to hire me, so I decided I could be just as fucked up and destitute in one place as the other, so off I went to Nashville. I was hoping I could at least find something there where I could make enough money to buy some clothes and a new guitar, since my old one seemed to have gone missing while I was gone. My daddy pawned it, I imagine. He probably got enough from it to maybe buy one cheap-ass bottle of whiskey.

Nashville wasn't exactly bustling with job opportunities—I mean, you couldn't just walk into one of those places on Music Row and tell somebody what a hot-shot guitar player you were and how you're maybe the greatest songwriter who ever walked the face of the earth since Hank Williams and expect something magical to happen just like that—but I was at least able to find a company that hired me for light janitorial duties. I worked at night six shifts a week with this other guy who was about half-deaf, so it didn't bother him much when I was working out my new songs out loud while I swept and massaged the floors. It was one of those big music companies down on Music Row, and sometimes in the mornings I could see the big execs coming in to go barricade themselves in their offices and try to come up with another hit for the airwaves.

I don't know how many songs I had in my notebook by then, but there was one in particular I couldn't file away for the future. It was a song called "Slow Burn," which I'd written in about twenty minutes while I was outside at two in the morning emptying trash into the dumpster. "Slow Burn" was this song about this guy who's found himself falling for this girl who he hadn't had much use for before, hadn't, in fact even noticed her much until all of a sudden she started showing up in his brain little by little a day at a time until she was a hundred percent in there and wasn't going to go away. It was a gem of a song, and no matter what I did I couldn't seem to improve it one bit from the original compilation. I knew this was the hit song I'd been waiting to come to me, and now the only problem was how was I going to get it out into the world for people to hear it?

Like I say, I certainly wasn't a prize when it came to attracting women, but I did get lucky somewhat in the fact that the person who gave me my weekly paycheck was a secretary in the lobby of this music company where I swept and mopped and polished floors and emptied trash those summer nights of 1972, and for some reason over the weeks she seemed to take a liking to me. Little stuff, like she'd always wave at me when I was leaving in the morning and smiled when she did it and for some reason, not like it always was with other women, it didn't seem like it was fake or she wanted something. Of course, I don't know what any woman might have thought some guy like me could possibly give her.

Anyway, one morning I stopped to talk to her. Just told myself to cross the line and take a chance, that the worst that could happen was she'd tell me to get lost.

Before I knew it, I was telling her I'd written "Slow Burn" just for her, and how someday I'd like to sing it to her. I wasn't even lying at the time, because the more I told her about it the more true it started getting. I even told her how for a couple of weeks by then I'd latched on to a small evening gig at a little pub called Lazenby's, where for twenty-five minutes a night I got to do a set and pass the hat around afterwards. It wasn't even my hat and sometimes I wouldn't even make five dollars from the show, but it was at least giving me the chance to perform and show off some of my songs in public. So I told Sharon—that was the secretary's name—about where I was playing before I came to work in the evenings, and lo and behold, she and two other women and one's husband showed up to hear me the next night. And the big thing about that was the husband turned out to be one of my building's producers.

His name was Justin Sloan, and right after I finished my set he asked me if I had a demo tape he could have, so I brought him a cassette tape I'd made in my apartment the next day. He smiled when he saw it and said he'd get back to me.

And the big surprise was in two weeks he did get back to me. He was waiting for me to do my nightly gig at Lazenby's on a Monday night. You didn't have a phone, he told me, so this was the only place I could think to catch you. I sure as hell didn't want to come down to the building at midnight and try and negotiate a deal with you.

A deal? I asked.

I want to sign you to a contract, he told me.

In two months "Slow Burn" was getting air time and Lazenby's was giving me choice times to perform every week and even paying me on top of what got put into the hat. Sharon and I were starting to keep steady company and life was going along better than I ever dreamed it could be. Two more months went by and I quit my janitorial job and started playing around town more, even getting booked as an opening act for the Oak Ridge Boys, so I was coming up in the world. I moved out of my fleabag apartment and found another one that actually had an extra bedroom in it, which seemed to me like the Taj Mahal after living in squalor the way I had for as long as I could remember. I got to thinking that life was finally going right for me and was going to stay that way, and I began getting visions about winning awards and living in a mansion with Sharon and driving a fancy sports car anywhere I went. I told myself how this was the good life and whatever I did I didn't need to screw it up.

"Slow Burn" made it all the way to #3 on the charts, and Justin got me in the studio and recorded five or six more demos of songs I wrote, certain there was another hit song in there so we could put together an album.

He released some singles but nothing caught on. It was like they'd all be around for maybe a week or so and then just disappear.

Nobody seemed to want to play them.

I look back now and I know I shouldn't have let it get to me so much. I should have been more patient than I was, but I got antsy and nervous and the next thing you know I was drinking like a fish and taking any pill or drug I could get my hands on. I wasn't any fun to be around either, and after about six weeks of me acting like a pig's asshole Sharon stopped having anything to do with me. I was out in the world alone again, and "Slow Burn" was rapidly becoming a thing of the past.

And I guess you know the rest, or if you don't, you can Google my name some time and read all about it—how I did my last set down at Lazenby's on a Labor Day weekend and drank myself silly before and during and after the show, and then like the fool I was went out and got in my Chevy and sped off down the street, going close to a hundred on the city streets before I wrapped myself and the car around a utility pole and crashed into the side of a bank. And that was it for me.

I was twenty-eight. That's as far as I made it. In a way I guess it was some kind of sad story, a tragedy of sorts, but I'm not going to lie about it. Maybe it was best that I went the way I did when I did, because I look back on it now and I think about the way I was and how I wasn't going to change anyway but for the worst, and how it was probably better for me to go before I was completely yesterday's news and was still on the radar of the music world the slightest bit. At least the way it is and the way it all went down folks will think of me now and then. It won't be like I'll be forgotten forever.

Hell, you start thinking about how my life had gone for the longest time until I hit the top with "Slow Burn," well, that's miracle enough right there. That's a lot more than I ever thought would happen. God was probably doing me a favor getting me out of the world before I had the chance to screw up any more of what might have come my way. I can't disagree with what happened one bit. I know how I am.

# PROSPECT GARDENS

## LINDA FAYE DORRIS
## (1941- 2022)
## THE LORD IS MY SHEPHERD

I don't think I ever wanted to be anything but a teacher my whole life. My mother taught fourth grade for I don't know how many years, and a good portion of my childhood was spent inside one of her classrooms, reading books from her school library while she graded papers or helping her put up bulletin boards or any number of things. I wonder how many times I went around her classrooms with a trash can throwing crumpled papers and chewed-up pencils away and getting the place halfway straight so poor old Cletis, the school janitor who was at least seventy years old, wouldn't have to work so hard because my mother's class consisted of a bunch of pigs. She was good that way. She always had prizes for the students every Friday if they'd done good during the week (and even if they hadn't) and she was forever bringing in Cletis a slice of cake or a big helping of pie, just because she was one of those people who could never stop caring about anybody.

I grew up wanting to be just like her. That meant being a teacher no matter what else happened in the future.

It turned out that Mama died before I ever got to be a real teacher with a certificate. I was still at college with a year left to go when she had a heart attack and died doing laundry in the basement, and she never got to see me in my own classroom with my own students following in her footsteps. Daddy lasted another six years, so he knew I'd been successful in graduating and teaching middle school English Comprehension, even though we still called it junior high in those days of the early sixties. Daddy was proud enough of me too, but it wasn't like him to want to come down to my school and see me in action; he may have done it when he was younger, but he was getting old by the time I got started and when Mama died he didn't go out that much anymore. He was fine if Les and I wanted to come by and visit, but most of the time he just liked fixing himself a sandwich morning noon and night and watching TV until bedtime. I think that was all he had left to live for, but bless his heart, because he never complained about it the first time.

Les and I got married about a month after I graduated from college. I was a June bride in 1962, and we had almost three years together before he went off to Viet Nam. He was three years older than me and worked in the drug store with Daddy as a pharmacist for four years. That's how we met. And then when Daddy retired Les took the pharmacy over. He was only about the third boy I'd ever dated by then, but we were really comfortable with each other right from the start. I was sad when he got drafted, but we made the best of it we could. We knew if we could make it a year or so everything would be all right.

And it was. The two total years Les was doing his military service I buried myself in my new role as a schoolteacher, and my first year I got assigned to a new school in a nice neighborhood, which was totally unexpected and out of the blue, but I certainly jumped at the chance when it was offered to me. I was assigned to teach two levels of Grammar and two of Composition and they even offered me the job of being in charge of the school paper and the annual along with another teacher, and I was glad to do that as well.

The teacher I would be working with on the paper and the annual was named Joanne Hopkins, and Joanne was just about in a carbon copy situation similar to me. She taught eighth grade lit and grammar, a year ahead of me, and she also had a boyfriend in the service too, the only difference being they weren't married yet. It turned out Joanne got her teaching degree from a Nazarene college on the other side of town, while I got mine from a state school thirty miles down the road, but we might as well have been twins, seeing how about all the courses we'd taken were close to identical. What with all that going on between us, it was natural that we became good friends almost from the beginning. We were always together at school and eating dinner at night and going to the movies and shopping together like we were joined at the hip. It was like she was the sister I never had.

My work day always began with my homeroom class that came in for roll call and announcements the first twenty minutes every morning. It was a big group of about thirty-five kids aged twelve and thirteen, and the girls were all in to acting grownup and the boys were wild and loud and always trying to out-do each other and show off for the girls. I'll bet the first two weeks I had to break up five fights before roll call ever got finished, and it got so bad that the boys basketball coach, Ronnie Grady, had to come over from next door and grab a few by the scruff of their necks and take them outside to get acquainted with his paddle. I didn't much care for that sort of thing back then, but I learned pretty fast that getting "knocked off" was par for the course during the school day. They never taught me that in college.

I suppose I was pretty impressionable in those early teaching days, because it seemed like when somebody would tell me something I would take it as gospel and go to the ends of the earth with it. I guess I was just so eager to please that sometimes I didn't exhibit good common sense. For example, when Joanne wanted us to go out with the teachers some afternoons after school and eat dinner and drink, well, I went with her even though I was uneasy about it. I had never tasted alcohol before except for once or twice at college, and I hadn't really over-imbibed on those occasions, so I wasn't totally prepared when these groups of eight or twelve faculty members all met in crowded taverns or dark pubs and everyone started ordering drinks like it was their last day on earth or something. Joanne got me to drinking a glass of draft beer and branching out each time to wine or hard liquor and finally frozen daiquiris, which I started to really acquire a taste for the more I had one. Pretty soon I was being driven home because I was tipsy and sometimes the experience was pleasurable and sometimes not. I got sick in a bathroom once and that was no fun at all.

And then there was the time when Ronnie Grady offered to drive me back to my car where it was parked in the school parking lot and before I knew it we had gone instead to a city park and he'd found a dark place to park his car and the next thing I knew he was all over me and before I knew it I was kissing him back and letting him put his hands anywhere he wanted. Nothing further than that happened that night, but I knew I was in a lot of trouble when I woke up that next Saturday morning remembering what had happened. I didn't know how to handle what happened the night before and what might be coming later. I only knew that I was a married woman and he was a married man and this was wrong. There was Les over in Viet Nam and here I was acting like a whore. I was really ashamed of myself and vowed I'd do better.

But I didn't do better.

I kept on seeing Ronnie off and on and sneaking around and thinking I had everyone fooled, but it turned out we weren't fooling anyone at all. Everyone knew about us, and the word soon spread to the main office and the principal, and the two of us got called in and told we could either both accept reassignments or tender our resignations, and that was it. I couldn't allow myself to have this on my record, so I took the job they offered me, which was in a poor section of town with students who looked like they had been in the penitentiary or were on their way there very soon. It wasn't exactly the situation I'd dreamed about and pictured myself in, but I'd done it to myself and I told myself I had to stick it out and pay the price for my mistakes.

I made it through the rest of the year and started teaching summer school when Les came home on leave. I was glad regular school was out and he wouldn't see where I was teaching now, and I did my best to keep my secret from him and take a step on a higher road for the future. I knew right then I'd never totally forgive myself for my infidelity and would carry it with me the rest of my life, but I vowed to myself I would from that day forward make certain

I would always do the right thing and make life for Les and me a blessed thing. I asked God for forgiveness and told myself to accept his mercy and then move on.

The good thing was life did get better right after that. I spent another two years at Marcella Best Middle School, and by working hard my test scores skyrocketed through the roof and the students all liked me, enough that by my second year there I got voted Teacher of the Year. Enough time had passed that the shadow of my past indiscretion had lifted and there were no long memories haunting my presence, and I soon got offered a position at one of the better schools in town. Rosa Parks Middle wanted me as a faculty member so much that I didn't even have to interview for the position. The principal called me up and offered me the job over the phone, saying he didn't need to interview me because he already knew I was the person he wanted for the job. You have quite the good reputation, he told me.

I was happy for a long time at school and at my church. My marriage to Les was fine for ten years or so and we had two children, a girl and a boy, by the time I turned thirty. All was well until Les made the same mistake I did and got involved with another woman who worked in the pharmacy with him. When the affair surfaced he told me it had only gone on for a month or so but I was never certain. He may have been downplaying how long he'd been cheating on me, but in the end I had to come to grips with myself and remember that I had made the same mistake years before, and I had never let him know about it because I didn't want to hurt him. This is what I told myself, but I finally had to face the truth and admit that the reason I'd kept it from him was to save my own skin and not have him know the extent to which his wife had sinned. I wanted to keep it a deep dark secret so I could uphold my standing and my reputation.

And I'm ashamed to say I never did tell him anything about it. I kept quiet about it until my dying day and lived in fear of being discovered for the rest of my life. Oh, it wasn't this big thing that consumed me and caused me to have an ulcer or anything like that, but I did have to do a lot of covering my tracks to make sure none of what happened ever came up. I put a lot of distance between myself and Joanne after I transferred—hardly ever even talking to her again—and anybody else I worked with at my old school I made a point to avoid too. It was like when I transferred out I disappeared off the face of the earth. I thought it was better that way. I knew I couldn't stand being around anyone who had an inkling of what had transpired between me and a married man, and so I buried that part of my past as deep as possible and made sure never to be in a position where I might meet up with someone who possibly knew all the gory details in my past.

Les died six years before me, and it was hard living my last years wondering if in the afterlife he knew what I had done. I had no idea how that worked, but it certainly gave me a lot of pause for thought until my time finally came around.

I still don't know. What I think is a person carries their secrets with them into the grave and no one is granted any special insight into what someone else had been up to in their private life, but all I can say is it's been two years now for me and I don't have the answer to that yet. Probably I never will.

I know it sounds like I was guilt-ridden all those years but that's not hardly true. I learned, like I suppose most everyone does in their lifetimes, how to live with myself and accept my shortcomings as well as my strengths. Nobody's perfect, you know, and it's probably just as well. It could be that if I'd never made a mistake in my life I would have become one of those pompous, lip-pursing women that my mother used to talk about having to tolerate. I might have never brought anyone any joy during my time on the earth, and that would have been sad. I much prefer it this way, because now I can look back on the students I taught and influenced, my children whom I raised to be good human beings, and the good marriage I scraped and constructed for Les and myself, even though neither of us were perfect all the time.

But we had a good life together. There were children and holidays and vacations and nice nights of having dinner and watching television. There was nothing to regret so much after the dust settled. I'm satisfied, see? I had a happy life in spite of myself. I learned how to negotiate the bumps and bruises and have a nice ride down the road before me. When you add it all up I don't think a person can ask for a whole lot more.

# REFLECTION RIDGE

## Martha Louise Green
## (1933-2012)
### TO GOD BE THE GLORY

All the time growing up and going to church I believed how it was going to be when I grew older. I knew the Holy Spirit was always going to watch over me and keep me from evil and wrong-doing, but if I got pressed I guess I'd say it hasn't necessarily been that way. Don't get me wrong. I had a good long life and made it to the cusp of my eightieth birthday, I had a good marriage until Ernie got lung cancer and finally passed away eleven years before me, and we'd had a beautiful daughter named Sarah Marie, who'd been the pride and joy of my life for thirty-three years. Yes, it was sad there toward the end when the drugs finally took her, and it had been a long struggle before that dark day came, but there had been joyous times before all that, and I have to keep that in my memory and not let the bad things rule my thoughts.

I first met Ernie when my family moved to Nashville from Little Rock, when I enrolled in Ellington High School as a sophomore in 1949. The war had ended four years earlier and my father had come home to my mother and my two brothers and me, and for a while he worked for the city in Public Works, or you might as well say a garbageman, which was a term Daddy never took too kindly to. He figured he was a veteran and deserved better, and maybe he did, but Little Rock certainly wasn't the town to rise above the rest of the working class and find your fortune in. Maybe it's better today, but it wasn't much of a good place to live back then.

Daddy had a brother, my Uncle Billy, who lived in Nashville and persuaded Daddy to move there and work at the Water Company with him, then, in their spare time, they could practice their musical act together and see if they could somehow get on the Grand Ole Opry. Uncle Billy played the banjo and Daddy played guitar and they sang as a duet. It never happened, and after maybe ten years they gave up that dream, but that was what brought us to Nashville to begin with.

Ellington High School was about the best place I'd ever seen. There were maybe a thousand kids going to school there from the ninth until the twelfth grade, which was more than twice as big as what I was used to before, and the buildings were new and there was a big football field where the football team was one of the best teams in the state year after year. Sports was not only a big thing for all the boys who went there but was important to the girls too. There were girls on the basketball team and the tennis squad and the track team, but most of the girls' first inclinations was to try out for the cheerleading team. If you were a cheerleader at Ellington High School in those days, well, you might as well say you were set for life, because you'd already been awarded a front row seat in heaven.

Well, I made the cheerleading team all right, mainly because I was quite pretty in those days and stood out from the other girls around me, but I was from a place before where I wasn't as accustomed to the ways of the world as this school I found myself in my sophomore year. Oh, I was smart enough and considered myself smarter book-wise than most everyone around me, but I didn't know about such things as dating or drinking or how far to let a boy go when you were out with him. Not only was I inexperienced and ignorant of such things, but my mother didn't help me along the least bit during that uneasy time. I don't know if she was ignorant herself about the ways of the world or had simply chosen to ignore the wicked goings-on around her and pretend her daughter would never get caught up in it like everyone else, but anyway, she never sat me down and discussed it or opened her mouth to give me any advice whatsoever. She just acted like none of it existed and there was absolutely nothing to worry about.

It turned out there was plenty to worry about. I found that out pretty fast.

Right off the bat I became quite popular with the boys in my class. It seemed to me the entire football team was always coming up to me and talking in the halls or calling me on the phone at night to ask me out for dates. For a while I had to turn them all down, because Mama and Daddy weren't allowing me to car-date just yet. I had to wait and be sixteen before that happened, and I was still a few months off. But that didn't stop some of the boys coming by my house and parking in the driveway and talking to me out on the front porch. They'd be out there every afternoon after football practice, or stopping me from going out to catch my ride home from Daddy after cheerleading practice. Some of them were really cute and nice and I had a hard time trying to decide which one I wanted to be my boyfriend when I finally became sixteen and could start dating. I didn't know then how boys can be so sweet and nice when they're after something they want, and I didn't know that I was the number one target on all the boys' list on who they wanted to get their hands on in a car or at some party. But I found out a lot of things as soon as I turned sixteen.

It was fun for a while. I went to movies and parties and cruised around with some cute guys in their cars after school and basketball and football games, and at first I thought it was all just one big fun ride until the time came when these boys wanted to take me parking and didn't want to take me home until I'd played around with them a while in their back seats, which I was bound and determined I wasn't going to do. I not only had high moral values from all my years of going to church but I was flat scared of those frightening moments too, afraid I'd lose my virginity and get pregnant and all my life would go up in flames, and so it got to be I turned down dates and stopped going to every party there was and soon afterward acquired the reputation of being a cold fish. I might have been one of the prettiest girls in school but that didn't seem to make anyone want to waste their time and money on dating me, because there was absolutely no reward for them in the end. That's the way it was by the time I reached my junior year. I was known as a goodie-two-shoes.

That's when Ernie came along. Ernie was a year older than me and was on the football and basketball teams and was always on the Honor Roll, and all I really knew about him was that he was quiet and shy and didn't go in for a lot of wild stuff like the other boys did. We met when we both got appointed to the Annual staff, and after a few weeks he called me and asked me out. We went to see "Harvey" with Jimmy Stewart and had a wonderful time, and that night was the beginning of our relationship. Two years later we married, and not long afterward Ernie was drafted to go fight in the Korean War. I was nineteen and a war bride going to college.

We made it through despite all the obstacles and setbacks I mentioned earlier, and it was in 1955 when our daughter, Sarah Marie, was born. That was when life was the best for me. My marriage to Ernie had overcome us being separated and being lonely and we were happy with each other. We moved to Athens to be closer to Ernie's family and soon I had a beautiful little daughter. My own parents were proud of me for becoming a mother and a schoolteacher, and I thought God had blessed me so that my life was going to be nothing but sunny from there forward.

And it was for the most part. Sadly, in two years I became pregnant again—this time a boy—but complications arose and after seven months his heartbeat stopped and I had to have a Cesarean delivery, which set me back both physically and mentally for a while. We named him and buried him in the children's section just down the hill, and up until the time I got sick I always visited him on his birthday and holidays and left flowers or a stuffed animal on his grave. I didn't want him to be forgotten.

Sarah Marie was good and healthy though, and she grew up even prettier than I'd ever been, which of course meant the boys started coming around like ants at a picnic. I had vivid recollections of my own teen years, and all at once I became this overbearing, protective mother who was determined to never let her daughter out of her sight long enough for some boy to enter in some secret passageway and ruin her life right at the onset. I thought I was totally justified in my actions, but soon I learned that all I was accomplishing was alienating Sarah Marie from me and giving her a reason to rebel.

And rebel she did. By the time Sarah Marie was seventeen neither I or her father could much do anything to control her. No number of threats or grounding or attempting to keep her in check did anything to stop her. She was wild and would go to any length to be free and ignore our wishes. She would stay out until the early hours of the morning and sometimes not come in at all. There was alcohol on her breath and drugs in her pockets, pills and marijuana and things I never heard of before and didn't know existed. It was as if I was getting a crash course education on what was out there in her world every day, and no matter what we tried we couldn't seem to stem the tide.

Finally it happened.

Sarah Marie drove into a guardrail on the interstate in her Volkswagen Bug at two-thirty on an early Sunday morning and was instantly killed. It was one of those cases where her blood alcohol was through the roof and her car was loaded with marijuana and drugs that she'd got from god knows where, and just like that her life was over and Ernie and I were childless. I guess I went to pieces during all that. I faintly remember making the arrangements or attending the visitation and funeral. I was in a daze the entire time and could hardly recall who came to the ceremonies whatsoever. There was a succession of her friends from school who came by, and all I can remember about any of them was how angry I was with them all, because in my mind each and every one of them had in some way contributed to Sarah Marie's death. They had either supplied her with the drugs or bought the alcohol or partied with her while she was on her way to the grave. They were the ones who had made it all happen. I cried a lot and said ugly things to some of them at one point, which was not like me at all. But I couldn't help it. My daughter was dead, and they had helped to make it happen.

There was one thing that stayed with me the most, and it

puzzles me to this very day. There was one boy who came to the visitation and the service by himself, and I recognized him as being someone who had once come to the house and picked Sarah Marie up for a date. I only saw him that one time, but I remember how polite he was and how he'd taken Sarah Marie to a movie to see "Wuthering Heights." Sarah Marie had hated it and said how corny and boring it was, but I was impressed that someone actually wanted to see something decent instead of all those sex and horror movies that were everywhere in those days. I guess the boy wasn't exciting or wild enough for Sarah Marie, because I never knew of her going out with him again.

But he'd come by the funeral home by himself. I remember seeing him standing off in a corner for a while, and then when I looked for him again he was nowhere to be seen until I spotted him at the service and later at the graveside service. All those times he never came up to either me or Ernie to say a word.

I didn't think about him for a long time. Life went on after Sarah Marie's death. I immersed myself in church and teaching and even volunteered one night a week at the Suicide Crisis Center.

I was eighty-one when I passed. It was my heart that failed me, but it didn't matter so much, as I was ready to go. Ernie and Sarah Marie were both gone before me, I'd long since retired from teaching, and most of my friends were gone too. I had gotten to the point where it was hard for me to drive, and rather than depend on other people providing me transportation, I simply stopped attending church or going out anywhere. The last two years I lived in the house I had my groceries delivered, and then I moved into a nursing home for my last eighteen months. The church gave me a nice funeral and what friends I had came by for the services, and afterward I found myself here on Reflection Ridge beside Les and Sarah Marie, and I am quite peaceful and at home here.

I don't know how it is for others who've passed on, but I don't communicate with anyone here in my proximity, not even my husband or daughter. What I do is reflect, like the area sign just down the trail tells me to do. I am very calm and serene, and nothing seems to excite me much or stir my interest in what the world I've left behind might be doing. It is all well with my soul other than one reoccurring incident that always gives me pause.

Perhaps it's not seven days a week, but more often than not a man comes walking this way. He passes by and always stops for a moment close to our plots, and it is as if he is taking a breath from a long trip and preparing himself to resume his journey. But he always stops here at the same place.

It has not taken me long to recognize him, even though it is many years since I first saw him. I do not even know his name, but his face is very familiar. He is the boy who took Sarah Marie to the movies that one night long ago, and whether Sarah Marie ever remembered him or not I do not know, but I did then and still do now.

He stops and looks upon her grave and is almost as if in a moment of prayer, and when he is finished he takes a deep breath and moves on. I wonder if he lives nearby, or if he makes a journey every time he can to visit Sarah Marie's grave. It is a long way from Nashville, but Ernie's family are all buried here and there is a family garden.

I wonder if Sarah Marie knows the things I do, and if she does, I wonder if the thought of this visitor is as blessed a thing to her as it is to me?

# SOLDIER FIELD

## JAMES LAWRENCE DeMARTINI
## (1949-1970)

### God Must Have Needed A Young Man

It seemed like a good idea at the time, right after I first thought about it and decided it was what I was wanted to do, but as soon as I followed through and signed up I knew I'd done gone and fucked up royally. It was like I quit thinking straight or something. I was so intent on pleasing my folks and getting out of harm's way there at home that I simply didn't consider the consequences of what I was getting myself into. At the time I was afraid I was going to end up in jail and how such a thing was going to screw up the rest of my life, but I didn't ponder too much what might happen once I got over to Viet Nam and had these asshole Viet Cong in pajamas taking shots at me. It was a whole lot damn worse than what I thought it would be. I just never gave much credence to the idea that I might end up dead and coming home in a body bag, which is exactly what happened.

I'm not going to take a lot of time going into my Viet Nam experience, other than to say it was awful and horrifying and as big a nightmare as I thought could exist in the world, and even though I died while I was doing it I still have to say that I'm glad I did because it at least put an end to what I was going through, so whether anybody believes me or not, in this case death was a relief and I'm glad it came along when it did because I was at that point where if something didn't happen to change things soon I was going to do something about it myself. I was going to make it end, even if I had to take my own rifle and do the job myself.

Just so nobody thinks I was completely crazy in the way I'm describing things, let me say that I'll talk a little about what possessed me to enlist into the service and enter into a certain version of Hell just to get away from the life I was leading before all that military shit came to be. A person might think things had to be bad in my life for me to do such a thing as enlist and go and make myself cannon fodder so a lot of billionaires in the country could get richer, but that's exactly the way it was. That's why it came to happen. It was like I was on a cliff being pursued by a pack of wild animals ready to rip me to shreds and devour me when they caught up with me, or I could take a leap out into the air and plunge to certain death down below me, like those poor guys King Kong shook off the log who fell down into a pit of giant spiders and got eaten. In my life it was either the wild animals or the goddamn spiders. Some fucking choice.

I didn't start getting in trouble until I hit middle school, but boy when I got started it was a race toward the finish line where nothing but trouble sat waiting on me to get there. I was constantly getting thrown out of classes and suspended from school and getting in fights for about a five year period, and then finally the public school system got sick of messing with me and sent me to this alternative place where I was surrounded with a bunch of no-good assholes like myself who couldn't for the life of them fit in with ordinary society in the least little way.

What got me sent to Green Hollow Alternative School was the result of me breaking in through a window and trashing the Biology Lab on a Thursday night, which all came down to me trying to get even with Mr. Anderson for flunking me the first six weeks of General Science my eighth grade year. It wasn't like I didn't deserve that big fat F I got posted on my report card, but it was more that everybody else in the class made As and Bs just by turning in their homework and paying the slightest bit of attention in class. Well, I did neither. I didn't do anything but sleep through every one of his classes, since they were held first thing in the morning at 7:30 for god's sake, too damn early to be worrying about why it rains or why the goddamn sun comes up in the morning and shit like that, and I never opened a book or studied or turned in what little homework got assigned. For everybody else it was a crip class, but I had no interest in sitting up straight and asking questions and acting like I gave a big shit. So I got my F. Sure, I deserved it and had it coming and all that crap, but it still pissed me off. It made me want to mess up Mr. Anderson's room and tear up his biology supplies so he and all his A students couldn't perform experiments anymore, or at least for a while. I figured I'd bust up some stuff and then go back out the window and go home and nobody would know any better.

Well, when I got ready to climb out there was already a cop car pulling up in the lot, and then when I turned around to find some other way out of the building I ran right into one of the two janitors the school had. This mother had been working all night waxing the gym floor and heard me tearing up stuff. I didn't even know he was around. It was just my luck. He grabbed me around the chest and wouldn't let go. He was a big, strong black guy who was about the size of an NFL tackle and I was no match for him.

Since I'd acquired the label of being nothing but a troublemaker over the past couple of years this act of destruction was the nail in the coffin for me. Back then a kid couldn't get away with as much as he can these days, because all you got then were three strikes and then you were out, banished from the real world and sent to some place like Green Hollow which was like one step up from the reformatory, so all you had to do was mess up a time or two there and you'd be carted off to the outskirts of town to a place called Salem Hills, where you lived in a dorm behind locked doors and a tall chain-link fence with barbed wire strung all along the top of it. Everywhere you looked you saw barbed wire and fences and padlocks. I knew all this, because my first day at Green Hollow they showed me pictures of the place and asked me if that was where I wanted to end up.

Green Hollow wasn't much better than the reform school. They didn't exactly keep us under lock and key, but they had a cop around with a big pistol on his hip and there was no way you could leave the building until a time-lock went off at dismissal time. You had to get on a bus or wait on a ride in alphabetical order, and they had to check you off a list before you could leave for the day. It was like you got a parole when the bell rang, but it wasn't like you were anywhere near free. You had to get used to getting watched all the time whether you were at school or not. When you got home you weren't allowed to go anywhere off your street and you had a curfew for when you had to be home before dark. It really sucked, you know. After a while you got to feeling like you were a prisoner in your own house, and how if you didn't learn to suck up and follow every rule you were going to stay that way forever.

I spent close to a year like that with no damn way to have any fun or see girls or anything but look at books and say yes sir and yes ma'am to a bunch of teachers I didn't like worth a shit, and then I ran away on a Friday night from my house and stayed missing almost a week until they caught me. I got nabbed stealing a package of bologna from a Kroger store and the cops came and took me in. They called my parents and the school authorities and everybody came down to the precinct station and collectively wondered what they were going to do with me. I told them I wasn't going back to Green Hollow and they said, fine, you can go to Salem Hills then, and after that, if that's not enough for you, you can go to the workhouse and maybe after that go to prison. Would you like that? No, I said, and I made like I was going to cooperate and do what they said, but the first chance I got I took off again, and this time I made damn certain not to get caught. I stole a car and got out of town and then hitchhiked far enough where nobody was looking for me.

It didn't work, though. One day I was just walking down a sidewalk and a cruiser pulled up beside me and two cops asked me where I was going and who I was. The next thing I knew I was in the back of the car and in a few days I was right back home again.

I made it clear that I wasn't going to go back to any alternative school, and I wasn't going to go back to Salem Hills or any regular school either, because I was turning sixteen then and if I wanted to drop out of school and find a job it was my decision to do so, because I was past the point where my parents could order me around and tell me what to do anymore. I hooked on to a job at a CB store about a mile from the house, and I walked to work every day to bag groceries and sweep and mop and perform whatever menial job they could find for me to do, and I hated every second of it but kept on coming in to work every day anyway, because I had it in my mind I was saving up enough to buy a car. And when I had a car I'd be out of there, the job, my parents' house, the whole goddamn town of Athens.

After a while they put me on the cutting crew unloading trucks and stacking cases of canned goods and cake mix and dishwashing fluid and anything else people go and buy in a grocery store, and though I was a skinny guy I still got stuck with the majority of the heavy lifting, and I don't have to tell you that got old after a while too. I kept thinking about what to do with my life long and hard until I finally decided to wait until I was eighteen and enlist, convinced like I was that anything would be better than what I was doing now.

So that's what I did. I figured out there was no way in hell I was ever going to save up enough money to buy a car, since my dad started making me pay rent to stay in the house, like he was going to teach me a lesson about quitting school and going out in the world without an education. I guess both he and Mama thought I was going to feel sorry about what I'd done sooner or later and see the error of my ways and start walking the straight and narrow like they wanted me to, but I guess I showed them. About a week before my eighteenth birthday I went downtown to the Army recruiting office to see what I had to do to join up. They told me to come back on my birthday with my birth certificate and Social Security card and they'd process my papers and see if I was eligible. I hadn't killed anybody yet so I thought it would be okay.

It was. They went ahead and swore me in and told me to come back in two weeks and report. And that was the end of my civilian life that had never done me the least little favor. I figured I'd go do my Basic Training and then one way or another I'd start serving my term as a soldier. I didn't know exactly what to expect, but it seemed pretty exciting to me. I had it in my mind I was going on a great adventure, which beat the hell out of what I'd seen from my own life so far.

It was an adventure, all right, but I wouldn't exactly call it great. I wasn't in Basic two weeks before some guy from Macon beat the shit out of me just for general principle, I suppose because he looked around at all the recruits and figured out I was the only one he could succeed in giving a beating to. It was something about me getting in his way in the showers, I never could understand exactly what, but he gave me a thrashing anyway. It might have been he got told to do it by somebody just so they could get rid of me before they had to go off to Nam, like I was such a shitty soldier and I was going to endanger everybody's life once we got over there, but I hung in there nonetheless. I was right there with my squad when we arrived to fight.

It wasn't like we did much fighting and killing any Viet Cong that much. Most of the time we waded through ponds and rivers and hid in bushes and listened to the sound of gunfire and bombs from far away from us, and generally it was the bugs and snakes that were our biggest enemies. We'd go a couple of weeks with nothing happening there at the beginning, and when something did go on where a gun actually got fired it was over in less than five minutes. Things were so quiet that first month there I started to believe that we were all going to die of boredom rather than get hit by a bomb or a sniper's bullet or step into some boobytrap mine and get our ass blown off. After a while I let my guard down and wasn't so scared anymore.

I remember about the last thing I was thinking about was what kind of car I was going to get me when I got home from all this, when we had some gunfire going on up ahead of us and on both sides, and everybody got under cover like they'd been taught to do, except I didn't see any place either on the riverbank or in the river that looked safe enough for me to hunker down in, so what I did instead was run up ahead to see if there was someplace better, which there wasn't, so after thrashing around in the jungle brush some I tried getting back to where everybody else was, and that's when a couple of bullets—I think it might have been three of them—went through my chest and my insides exploded all over the place, intestines and guts and blood and all that, and I fell down beside the river and that was it. I was dead.

They fixed up the record like it was the enemy who shot me,

but I really think it was friendly fire. I think I came up on some guys who were hiding in their positions and they thought I was a gook. They fired their weapons before they knew who was there. I can't prove it, though. It doesn't really matter. I'm dead, and there's no changing that. Wherever the gunfire came from, I'm a corpse either way.

I look back at it now and realize it's probably the only time in my entire lifetime I did anything to please my folks. The Army, of course, made it look like I was some sort of a hero and sent a letter of commendation and a flag home with me to the states, and when it came time for the funeral they had a contingent of officers and enlisted men there to give the eulogy and carry my casket out here to my plot. They even played Taps at the end of the burial service, and on top of that the military paid for everything, so my folks didn't have to shell out a penny. I was a hero and not going to cause any trouble anymore, and they didn't owe anybody anything after all the loose ends got tied up. Their son was resting in peace as a fallen hero, and they could finally relax.

So, here I am for the past forty-something years, waiting to see if I'm going to Heaven or Hell with nothing giving me an answer so far. I'm just here, watching others go by getting carried to their reward, people stopping by graves to lay flowers or a holiday deco-ration, and every now and then my mother comes by—Daddy's dead himself now—and she stands for a minute in silence. Sometimes people see my tombstone and leave pennies on top of it. Every now and then somebody will leave a quarter because I died in combat, or so they think. I didn't know such a tradition existed until I got here. And I don't know if Mama is praying for my soul or not, or if by now she's given up on the idea that Salvation might come my way after all. I guess after a while a person gets tired of waiting on something they know is never going to happen.

# TRANQUILITY VIEW

## CAROLYN MARIE VAUGHN
### Born: April 18, 1938
### Died: March 9, 1994

## Our Father Which Art in Heaven

I'm not really certain when it was I began to know I was different, because I never did have the kind of mind that documents dates and times when important events occur, but it was sometime during my early grammar school days, when all my classmates were busy having secret boyfriends and crushes and started passing notes with boys and talking about boys with one another. I sat there in the classroom at my desk and felt it going on around me, and when it was time for recess I never wanted to huddle up with any of the girls and talk about girl things but was a lot more interested in playing kickball and seeing if I could boot a ball over the fence like some of the boys could, or if I could play dodgeball and throw the ball hard enough that it would make a resounding whack sound when it hit somebody in the back or shoulder. I didn't want to have anybody think I threw like a girl, because even if I was a girl, I was learning early on I didn't want to act like one. I didn't have the slightest bit of interest in anything that involved being a girl.

I never seemed to come off that feeling and no one ever made much mention of it. I'm sure everybody noticed I never had a boyfriend or spent a lot of time dressing up to look nice, because most of the time I stayed busy playing all sorts of sports all the way through school. I played basketball in the winter and softball in the summer—fast pitch, once I got old enough for it—and I ran track in the spring and was pretty darned good at all of it. I could sprint and run long distance, I could perform low and high hurdles, and I'll bet I could have thrown a shot put or soared way up on a pole vault if I got the chance, but there were only twenty-four hours in a day, and there were times when I had to sleep and eat and go to school. For a while I joined a swim club and raced and executed high dives and somersaults off the diving board, but I couldn't stay with it as much as it required, because, like I said, I was involved in so many other athletic endeavors that there wasn't any way I could be in two places at once. I was good at what I did, though. I was All-City and All-State in both basketball and softball, and when I graduated I had scholarship offers from at least ten schools.

Like I said, all this time I didn't have much to do with boys, at least not in the boy-girl holding hands and stealing a kiss at the front door kind of way. I think I had maybe two dates during my high school career, and both were with the two offensive tackles on the football team, big oafs who weighed close to three-hundred pounds who were dumb as rocks once they got off the football field. Nobody else even asked, even though I was not bad-looking compared to the girls in my class. I didn't bother much with makeup or fancy clothes, so I suppose the boys all came to think of me the same way I did, maybe not as one of them so much, but just not quite the kind of girl you want to take to a movie or drive with to a dead-end road and make out with for an hour or two. It just wasn't that way at all, and I didn't mind it a bit.

As a matter of fact, I don't think I ever got my hormones all hot and bothered and lathered into a state until one night during my Junior year at Middle Tennessee State, where I was attending on a softball scholarship, on a Saturday night at a dorm party when I started a conversation with this bespectacled girl from the English Department after we'd both had our share of alcoholic spirits during the night's revels. Her name was Glenda Something—like the good witch from Oz, she told me—and we were standing out on a porch with our drinks talking about school and listening to all the loud music going on inside the house that was filtering out through the open windows. Before I had much of a chance to consider what was going on this Glenda had her arm around my neck and was pulling me toward her so she could administer a big, sloppy, tongue-wiggling kiss right out of the blue. I'd never had anything like this occur before and so I went into about fifteen seconds of profound shock, after which I found myself liking what was going on and wanting to continue to see what happened next.

Well, the truth was not much. We just kissed for maybe five more minutes and then we stopped like our allotment was up for the night. We didn't go find a room somewhere and get naked and do Sappho things I had no idea existed or anything like that; we just had maybe another drink or two and then said goodnight and went back to our own dorms. I didn't call Glenda later and Glenda didn't call me. It was just one of those things, like Maurice Chevalier sang about in that movie Gigi my mother took me to one time at the classic movie house in downtown Fayetteville when I was a little girl.

But that was the extent of my wanderings into the world of same-sex attraction, and it came to me later on that maybe I was one of those people who was AC/ DC, or maybe I didn't have any sexual inclinations at all, I was asexual or whatever you call it, and as I went along I found the only people I liked being around that much weren't people at all but dogs and cats. By the time I graduated and was working for a living and had saved up enough to buy a little house out in the suburbs I was the owner of three dogs and four cats, and we all lived together in my two bedroom house with a corner lot and a fenced-in backyard.

I'd used my softball scholarship to get my degree in Physical Education, and I came back home and got a job at South Unity Elementary School, which is where I attended back in my early schooldays. Even though it was an older school not too many famous people had ever passed through the doors before, and so the fact that I had actually won a scholarship to a big college and had played softball and basketball there was like a big deal to everybody in town, and so I got hired as a playground supervisor and spent my work days walking around in shorts with a visor on my head and a whistle hanging around my neck. About all that was required of me was to develop some sort of continuing physical health agendas for the grades One through Four and have students participate in assorted programs to earn their grade letters. There was running and volleyball and softball and basketball the kids could pick from, and at the beginning of every class I was supposed to lead them in five minutes of stretching and side-straddle hops and running around the gym twice before breaking off to individual groups. At first I tried to get serious with my efforts and go all-out making sure the kids of South Unity were physically fit, but after a while I could see how the whole idea was worthless and wasn't worth the time or the effort. That's when I started shooting basketball and reading People Magazine most of the day. When three-fifteen came around I was out in my Falcon and headed for home for the night, where me and my seven critters would fix dinner and watch television until bedtime.

It wasn't exactly an exciting, fulfilling existence I had going, but it was okay. It beat the heck out of working in a bank or working customer service for the water department. That's the way it was for most of the people in town, so I guess I was one of the lucky ones.

On a regular basis, on Friday nights I went to my parents either to eat dinner there or for the three of us to go to Captain D's and eat a fish dinner, and after a while I noticed that they didn't say anything anymore about when was I going to get married or if I had a boyfriend or anything like that. I think they'd given up on me providing a grandchild for them, which I knew they wanted desperately, since my little brother had gotten himself killed in a car wreck back when he was seventeen. He was four years behind me, but I think he was the one they held out hope for, because I'd never once exhibited any inclination to join in with the rest of the girls my age and have a husband and a home with kids everywhere you looked. I almost wondered if they could trade out one kid for another with one living and one dying they'd probably pick Billy, but I didn't dwell on such a penny ante idea like that much, because my parents did love me and it wasn't their fault I'd turned out the way I did. They were the ones who were normal and I wasn't. That's just the way it was. Nobody needed to feel bad just because things hadn't turned out the way it did on Happy Days. Sometimes that's just the way things go.

Daddy died on a July night in 1980. I don't like to dwell on it too much because it was on the night before my birthday the next day, and every year after that was like a week-long downer for me, my daddy dying and me getting older with no real purpose in my life other than to get through the day without a disaster happening. My mother wanted to sell her house and move in with me but I had cats and she was allergic to them. I guess I could have gotten rid of them and just had dogs but I didn't want to. See, not to sound like a weirdo or anything, but my pets were my friends. I didn't really have anybody close I could talk to or go out and eat with or see a movie. Since college and after I moved back home I never felt much of a need to call anyone up on the phone to talk or suggest going out someplace or go on some kind of vacation together, because I knew that after about ten minutes I'd have nothing more to say to them and wouldn't for sure want to listen to what they wanted to talk about. I liked my conversations with my dogs and cats better. Everything was pleasant and there were no implications to be pondered or hidden meanings to define. It was more like what could we all do to get cozy and enjoy being safe together, not any of us out there in the cold cruel world getting abused by people who didn't care if we were happy or sad or living or dead.

So I put off having my mother move in with me, and after a couple of years of that she found new friends and got more involved with her church and the danger was over. Lots of times we'd just talk on the phone because she wasn't available on Friday nights anymore—she was always at Game Night at her church—and there were lots of times I'd come home on Friday afternoons and not talk to a single soul until Monday morning of the next week. Sometimes it scared me that I was becoming such a hermit, but when I considered the alternative and imagined myself out somewhere in the thick of ordinary and very normal people I was more than happy to fix myself dinner and feed the animals and watch Family Feud or

Let's Make A Deal or Wheel of Fortune on the Game Show Network until I fell asleep on the sofa, then go to bed feeling thankful I was by myself and didn't have to perform any sexual maneuvering for whatever sexual partner I might be cursed with having around.

I know this sounds terrible, like I hated the human race or something, which I don't; I actually liked a lot of my students and had some who'd moved on to high school and college occasionally come by the school to visit me, which was fine. I was glad to see them. But there always came a time when I wanted them to go away and disappear back into their futures and leave me back in my own present where I simply didn't have to sweat being who I was. As long as I didn't have somebody coming along trying to rock the boat, I was fine. As long as it was peaceful and predictable I was sure I could go on living that way forever.

But the problem is you don't live forever. You can be peaceful and unencumbered and happy in your situation but there comes a time when your lease is up and you realize you don't get to go on that way for eternity.

The first unsettling thing that came my way was a mole on my upper leg that seemed to me to be growing, so I put it down in my head that on the upcoming spring break I'd go in and see my GP and see what she had to say about it. That was a month off and I thought I'd be just fine until then, but on occasions I started feeling incredibly tired and sometimes at night I started running a fever. I'd never had anything like that go on with me before, so it was then I started to get concerned. I made an appointment and went in the next week, and before I could argue about it Dr. Blanton had me scheduled for an Xray and several screenings. I had to miss a couple of days at school, which practically never happened, so everyone at school started getting ideas that maybe something was going on with me.

Anyway, I started losing weight by the bunches, so I knew something was wrong and pressed the doctors to tell me exactly what I was facing. After a lot of hemming and hawing around I was finally diagnosed with a form of pancreatic cancer, although at that early stage no one could say exactly if I had Exocrine tumors or the rarer Neuroendocrine. I was going to have to have a biopsy and surgery at some point and had it emphasized to me that my situation was going to get worse before it got better, that I was in for a lot of pain and stress over the coming months. What I had was extremely aggressive, they told me, and so we have to be aggressive right back in the treatment. You'll not only have surgery but probably chemotherapy and a lot of drugs. After a while you'll have to take a leave of absence from your job. Your hair is likely to fall out, and you're going to need a caregiver of sorts to look after you at times. It is not going to be easy.

I couldn't get through any portion of the day without the thought of what was happening within me overtaking anything I was trying to do, being in the gym, watching a movie at home, or just sitting outside on my patio with my pets, the idea was always in my head. Radiation, surgery, removing tumors, determining if something was benign or was spreading, it was consuming and frightening. I was angry because I'd always been healthy all my life. I could run and jump and beat practically anyone in any physical competition there was, but now it seemed like I was being controlled by a battery that was low and running down and soon all the wonderful physical activity I'd always engaged in would be impossible for me to do, and I spent all my time attempting to learn to cope with such a stark reality. Was I going to die very soon? Was I going to leave this world long before I'd ever planned to? How was it possible the world could go on without me? Who would replace me at school? Who would take care of all my animals?

I started doing weird things. I visited my mother three or four times a week and talked about anything but my cancer. I talked about how we could go on a cruise together and how maybe I would start going back to church with her every week, although none of that ever happened. She didn't know how bad my condition was because all I ever told her was that the doctors were pleased with my progress and expected me to be all right pretty soon, cancer-free and all that malarkey. I lied so much to her about my condition that pretty soon I almost started believing it myself.

After several months of treatment from A to Z—believe me, I ran the gamut—the belief came to me that no matter what the doctors tried and what I went through during the treatments it was all going to wind up the same way in the end anyway. That's when I started taking my pets to the rescue shelter one at a time. I couldn't just load them all up in my car and take them in all at once, because it was heartbreaking as hell enough doing it a little at a time. I had five cats and four dogs by this time, so what I did was give them away by seniority, the youngest first and the oldest last. I guess I was hoping I'd die before I was left all alone in the world with none of my furry friends around me. It was one thing leaving my students and my faculty friends and my mother behind, but it was another to be without my brood, who were always the most precious living things to me. I wanted to make certain there was someone around to take care of them the way I always had.

At first I was so angry at the world and myself and God—if He was up there, which I was struggling to believe—that I spent a lot of time cursing Fate for treating me this way. I told myself that the great big world was out there spinning around and how everything was going to go along fine without me when I was gone, and I was fuming that there was so much out there and I was never going to see it or be a part of it. Then I was mad at God for making me the way I was. I didn't have a husband or children or even a partner to help me through this journey toward the end of life, and I wanted to know why it was me He chose to be different while everyone else in my sphere had a happy life going. They were normal and I was anything but.

But most of all I was upset with myself. Deep down I knew I didn't have anyone to blame for my wasted life but myself. I was the one who chose to keep to myself and spend my days and nights alone. People had reached out to me all my life and tried to get closer, but I had done nothing but push them away and keep them at arms-length. It was like I had made a concentrated effort to keep the world at bay so I wouldn't get hurt or have to explain the way

I was. I should have tried coming to grips with my feelings and charting a different path just so I could be open and free to live my life the way I wanted and do and go as I pleased without having the overwhelming urge to take cover and hide so I wouldn't be found out, but it was like I froze up and never tried to do a thing about any of it. It was as if I was guilty of a crime and I didn't really know how to classify or rectify it.

The cancer made quick work of me. It didn't take a year until I was in the hospital and then carted off to a hospice care unit, because there was nothing else anyone could do for me. I was just there to wait it out until the end came, however long that took, and it was time for me to get my affairs in order. The only thing was I didn't have any affairs. My pets were all given away and my color television was back at my house, waiting to be sold with my clothes and kitchen utensils when the estate sale got held. I knew it would be a one-day affair. Like my personal life, I hadn't accumulated much to speak of.

I passed away a little over a week at the hospice. I remember my mother coming in several times, and how she brought her preacher with her the last time. I had lain there the whole time with my eyes closed, not sure if I was sleeping or too weak to talk or simply hiding again. I was so good at keeping things distant that I did it right up to the very end.

The funeral was a sad little affair with only a few people present. The school sent a wreath and some of the teachers came by for visitation. Most of the people were from my mother's church. It had been so long since I attended services I hardly knew any of them.

I've been here twenty-five years and plus now. It's quiet and nothing is required of me. I don't know if I'm waiting to go to Heaven or what the deal is. All I know is being in this place is not really so bad. I guess that after a while you can get used to anything as long as it's not too terrible, or at least that's the way it's always been with me. Out here nothing's required of me, and I can stay here by myself and think about anything I want. I don't have to plan anything or worry about pleasing anyone anymore, as if I ever did such things anyway. So it's like it's all just more of the same. It's almost like it's heaven to me this way, and it's all just fine this way. Some people might not like it, but they're not me. I like it just fine the way it is. It helps to keep everything uncomplicated.

# DARKNESS

When the living are home from work and sitting down to dinner or perhaps on the road to a favorite dining place, when the rush hour is passed and the streets can be freely driven again without the stops and gos and horns honking and the occasional fist clenched or threats exchanged and the possibility of violent road rage coming around, that is when the creatures come out from their hiding places, their burrows, their dens, their nests, their crags, and begin to wander Summer Haven for food and foliage and perhaps heed the call of a possible new mate. Twilight and dusk envelop the grounds, and beneath the rising moon and the appearance of stars and constellations the world of Summer Haven becomes non-human for a time.

The resting inhabitants of Summer Haven do not qualify in the human category anymore. They are not human now, but of another persuasion that none of the living creatures settled here are very sure about.

Hawks pick this time to rest, to find a place among the many trees to repose a while, since they have been busy most of the day soaring and swooping and studying the earth below for morsels of flesh they can take for food for themselves and the hatchlings in their nests. Squirrels look for cover at this time, since they innately know the hour has come for them to be stalked, for it is now when the coyotes appear, the predators supreme, who know no limits when it comes to the nightly hunt. The fox is along for the hunt too, but steer clear of the packs of coyote that would as soon turn on them as prey and make a meal of them too. The deer nose out from hidden thickets and woods, ready to eat and perhaps mate but wary of the hunters who might be picking up their scent. At certain times of the year Canadian Geese honk and amble about in packs eating insects and grass, staying together as a cohesive group in case one of them is threatened and the need for a group attack becomes necessary. When threatened the geese become dangerous creatures. Now and then the occasional bobcat comes forth to reveal himself.

The darkness is a time for boldness and freedom, for the main enemy, the human beings, are not present at this time. They are apart and away in their own domiciles and not a threat to the animal community at this time. It is not so much that these beings come with destruction on their minds, but it is just the fact of their presence, their voices, their metal conveyances spewing fumes and smoke, slamming doors and racing engines. There is also the matter of their scent, which does not invoke prey or kinship but essentially denotes a lack of privacy and a sense of possible danger. It is because of this scent that the men mowing lawns and driving bulldozers and digging more graves to deposit their dead come around the days of the week to perform their duties, to do their job, to subtract more and more of the homes and hiding places of the night creatures residing at Summer Haven.

But in the night the presence and noise and scents of these living usurpers are gone. This is the time the animals know it is safe to emerge and re-claim this portion of the earth that is daily being taken from them. Yes, there are still human remains present, but there is something about these human beings who being dead have not the same dangerous manners about them anymore. They do not walk about or plunder or dig or perform any of the threatening things their daily survivors execute; they are quiet and repose and make no sounds at all, emit no trace of life's aroma whatsoever.

The creatures are accustomed to those who rest here in their graves, in their vaults and boxes and coffins beneath stones and spheres and marble markings. Unlike the living who come during the day, the dead at night make no movement, emit no noise, are present only to remain at some sort of rest and achieve a state of peace, unknowing, silent, asleep in their private eternities to co-exist with the night beings forever. The longer these dead slumber, through weeks and months and years, the more the animals become comfortable with their presence. The deer know the denizens of Paradise Vista, the coyotes hunt by Hillside Estates, the racoons forage within Rockabye Valley. Perhaps those souls interred here are aware of their nightly revels, but it is like there is a treaty between the animals of the night and the earthly remains of those who rest at Summer Haven.

Occasionally a fox barks or a coyote howls. An owl may hoot and a doe will meet a buck in a tryst, but there are no loud explosions, no gunfire or angry voices. There is only the rhythm of the night, food being gathered and the species being continued and the beating of hearts beneath a sky full of stars, a moon holding court until the birds proclaim the coming of the dawn.

# ORPHAN LAWN

## THOMAS DANIEL GRAY
## 1954-1961
## The Lord is My Shepherd

**W**hen you're here at Summer Haven you never grow up. Half a century and more I've been out here and I'm still seven. It's not so much I'm still seven in my mind or anything like that, because when you're in one place you have a lot of time to think and more than enough minutes of the day to watch people come and go and see how they're dressed and what kind of car they're driving. After a while you get to where you know if people are happy or sad or good or bad. You know if somebody's genuinely sorry that someone has died or if deep down inside they're glad someone in particular is gone and out of their sight for good. Though not very often, there are still times when people show up around here who have a lot of mischief and hate in their hearts and write dirty things on markers or turn tombstones over just for fun. It doesn't go on very much—I've seen stuff like that happen two or three times during my years here—but it gets to where you start thinking how any time now somebody's going to come around and cause trouble. It worries me at times. I for sure don't want anybody coming up and messing with my plot just because they know I'm an orphan and the evil in them wants to go on picking on somebody who spent their entire lifetime being unhappy and expecting the worst. It's like being lonely and sad during my real life has carried over to this one. People think when somebody like me, an orphan, dies that things will get better for me once I cross over. Well, they're wrong. I've been right here in this place for as long as I ever expected to live in the first place and I haven't so much as glimpsed Jesus coming my

86

way yet. They've got a statue of him right here out in front of the Orphan Cemetery section, and He's sitting on a rock with a lamb on one side of him and a little kid in His lap, and the inscription says "Suffer the little children to come unto me." I don't mean to act ugly but I haven't seen anything like that out here yet. It's just me here day and night and rain and shine with the months and years going by, all by myself waiting on I don't know what to happen, and I haven't seen anybody yet that I could actually go to.

One thing's for certain. It's hard for me to come unto Jesus because I haven't had the first sighting of Him yet.

It would be nice, I suppose, to have a mom and dad and maybe a sister or brother to come around and mourn me now and then, to maybe stand here in front of my stone and say a prayer or something in my memory, but I haven't ever had anybody around to do anything like that, so I don't really know if I'd appreciate it or not. The thing is I don't even know who my real parents were. I have no idea if they're even still alive or anything like that. See, I was given up when I was about one or so, so I don't remember the first thing about what my parents even looked like. And being as young as I was when I died, I never got around to asking anybody any details about who I was or where I'd come from. Most of the time all I remember is simply being sick from the measles and being in a hospital for a long time. I don't know how I got it, but a lot of kids at the orphanage got sick at the same time, and it was like there was an ambulance at the orphanage doors all the time for about a month. This was just before the vaccine came out, so it was pretty serious at the time. Kids had to go to the hospital and stay in beds in an isolation ward surrounded by hundreds of other sick children. There were lots of cases of diarrhea and vomiting going on, and some of us were even so unlucky as to developing further symptoms on top of the measles. A lot of them could be pretty bad.

I was one of the unlucky ones. I picked up an infection in my lungs that developed into pneumonia.

I was sick for weeks. I stayed in this room by myself for a long period of time, the only people I saw being doctors and nurses who kept coming in and giving me shots and pills and hooking me up to machines that made it easier for me to breathe. One of the few things I remember was the day when they came in and said it was my birthday and tied balloons to the railing of my bed and gave me a cookie with a candle in it. About six people stood around the bed and sang Happy Birthday to me but I fell asleep before they finished. I was that bad off.

I don't have anything bad to say about the hospital staff that waited on me for so long, because they did the best they could with what they had. At the time there was no real vaccine for measles, so whoever got it just had to wait it out and hope for the best, and I just happened to be one of the few that didn't get any better on my own but just progressed into worse things, like pneumonia. I think I also developed a case of encephalitis, although nobody ever really came out and said it for sure, probably because there were so many other things going on with me that it was hard to single out one specific symptom. I was coughing and my eyes were swollen and red and on top of everything else my ears got infected. I guess probably five or six different doctors got called in to look me over and see what they could do, but in the end it didn't do any good. I passed away three weeks past my seventh birthday.

Of course, I never really knew what my official birthday was. I think whenever it was I arrived after my mother gave me up somebody just picked out a date and put it on my chart. Maybe they had a birth certificate somewhere, but I'm not so certain about that. Like I say, I never had time to investigate or ask anyone about where my mother was or who she was or why she hadn't wanted to keep me. I just went on what I got told. By the time I was old enough to ask questions I was too sick to talk. It was all I could do to stay conscious.

One night I went to sleep and didn't wake up. I know it sounds strange but I was aware of everything that was going on around me, nurses hooking me up to machines and doctors giving me shots and trying to revive me, but there wasn't anything I could do about it. All those people were alive and where they were, while

I was dead and gone and in a place where they couldn't reach me anymore. After a while they stopped trying and I knew I wouldn't be staying at the hospital anymore. I'd be going somewhere else. At the time I was still too young to have any idea where that might be.

It wasn't much of a funeral at all. There were two people from the hospital, some kind of official and a nurse, and two people from the funeral home, and they all stood around while this preacher they'd brought in from somewhere said a few words and read the 23rd Psalm, and then that was it. The next thing I knew we were all loaded up in a big van—they didn't even use one of those black funeral hearses—and we rode down a couple of lanes until we got to the section where all the orphans ended up, those of us who didn't have a soul called family who'd be around and possibly genuinely sorry that one of us had died. Where we stopped didn't even have a pretty name like all the other sections around the cemetery did. There was just this sign that read Orphan Lawn, like it was just a yard where kids like me came to get dumped. At the time I was still too young to read the word "orphan," since I'd been sick so long I'd missed most of First Grade and all of Second, so at first I wasn't sure what this meant. I learned really fast though, especially when they started lowering me into this hole in the ground and I figured out what they were doing. I wanted to cry out and bang on the top of the casket for them to not go through with this, to let me out, but after a minute I knew I wasn't able to do anything like that anymore. This was maybe the first time I started to understand what it meant to be dead, how it was a whole new world I was entering into at this stage.

Believe it or not, I've learned a whole lot of things since I've been here. I know the general thought is that once a person's heart stops beating and all the bodily functions that accompany life quit working then it becomes impossible for that person to acquire knowledge or be privy to any experiences anymore. Maybe that's true for those who've had their allotted years and done their due time on earth among the living, but for people like me who didn't get a chance to do much of anything at all there's something present—and I don't know where it comes from—that allows us to stay tuned in and soak up what is going on in the world each day without us. Take me, for example. I learned to read just by looking out from my plot at the other tombstones around me, working out the letters of the names into sounds I remembered from my early few months of school, and after what amounted to years I was able to know people's names and how to pronounce them. Now and then people or traffic would go by my vision and I could hear them talking or their radio playing in the car and I'd pick up a lot of things in passing like that. I could see how the cars changed shape with each year, how every model was different and more advanced, and though it was that no one who was out here dead ever spoke to me—we dead don't exchange conversations because we're in worlds of our own— there still was and is a lot of energy floating around in this place, leftover intimations from lives gone away with unsaid words they'd wanted to say still hanging around waiting to go into an ear that can no longer hear it. There are all the senses still present in me, still alive although I am dead, and it's things like that hovering in my aura that keep me involved all day. I suppose eventually I will absorb as much of this data as I can muster, and that is when I will go to the next stage of my being, but like death is to the living, I don't know what that is just yet.

I do have one reoccurring thing going on that I've yet to be able to understand. About once a month, always on a Sunday afternoon—yes, I am still able to determine the days of the week, the month, the year—a woman appears before my grave after she's embarked from what looks to me a black Honda Accord, although she parks so far away I am not certain this is the model. She takes leisurely steps along two pathways and finally stops before my grave. She does not bring flowers or say anything aloud; all she does is stand for a moment and gaze at my stone, as if there is some connection between us and she is saying some sort of prayer to God to provide us a connection. The thing is I am a hundred percent certain she is not my mother and is no kin to me, but none of that stops me from wondering what it is that brings her here this way.

I have absorbed a great many things about the world in my state of self here these years; I am not just a poor, hapless unfortunate child who never had the opportunity to see what the world had to offer, but I have yet to figure this riddle out.

But maybe I have. In the past several months a voice has come into my head and urged me to stretch my memory and see if there is something familiar about this lady. How old is she? Does she live in this area? Have I ever seen her before? If she is not from my unknown family is she someone I have come in contact with at some time? The idea continues to formulate and seems to be coming to me.

I think she is my mother's friend. It seems to me she is on a mission of sorts coming here each month like this. Perhaps my mother was forced to give me up through no fault of her own, and maybe this lady is the friend who was around and tried for so long to comfort her. A goodly part of me wants to believe her appearance here is the result of a death bed promise made to my dying mother, that she would always look after me in the years to come. But I cannot be assured of that. It could be this woman is the friend of a deceased mother who had no idea where her surrendered child was, that she never knew and her friend never knew, but now this friend is fulfilling the deep chasm in her dead friend's life by coming here to Orphan Lawn and picking out my grave as a symbol of another lost and solitary child, and so I am a symbol of heartache and loneliness that was her friend and her child. Perhaps I have assumed that place in the hole of broken hearts, and, if so, I suppose that is all right with me. In a way it fills the void in me too. It is heartening after all this time. It makes me feel there is a purpose to my existence after all that has happened.

But this mysterious woman and her monthly visits are all I have to do directly with the world anymore. Whatever there was of it, which was sparse and short-lived, is gone from me for good now, so what I am is merely an observer, a watcher of what manner of life passes by each day. Perhaps it is a member of the human race, a visitor or a walker or a vandal, maybe it is only passing vehicles going by the main road in front of me to visit some other loved one's grave, but most of the time it is only the animals connecting me to the world anymore, crows and hawks and deer and coyotes, all of whom venture by here in the dead of the night to pry me from the long hours of darkness and solitude where I can't help but revert back into my seven-year-old state and am afraid and cowering about being forever alone and want something to come along and save me. It is not so bad as it was at first, all those years back, but the fright still returns some nights and I feel it all the same as before. I wonder if it will ever stop.

I guess what I've been trying to say is no matter how much time passes and what goes on before me the bottom line is I'm always going to be here in my place however much the world changes, who is born and who dies. Whether I move on eventually to another state doesn't matter; a part of me will always be here. I'm not going anywhere in that regard. I am here as someone's child, a woman, a man, the three of us never united after a certain stage, and whether they have entered my place now or not is of no consequence. The thing is once we were all of the living world together at one time, and no matter how long eternity lasts there will always be that history of us remaining. What happened between us caused a change in the world at some certain small point, and because of that change each of our lives on earth were altered forever. That is something that will never change.

It is strange how in so limited a life that so much baggage accompanies me in this afterlife. It is strange that in so little time I could carry so much with me. I think about it quite a lot. It makes me wonder. It's not clear if I'll ever figure everything out completely. But I have a lot of time. That's the thing. There's never going to be any hurry or deadline for me to meet with the answer. For me, time is one of those things that will never be up. For that I don't have to worry. I'll be here until I'm not. The sun comes up and the sun goes down, and I'll be here watching. I suppose there's something good to be said about that. I can at least know my worries are over in one sense while I wait for something new to come along.

# GOOD SHEPHERD ESTATE

## MARTIN BRANDON GARRISON
## (1913- 1984)
## GONE TO GOD

I can't say that it's all that different these days, me being here in my grave every day and every hour like it is now, than what it used to be before, when I was the caretaker of this place and I had a nice rock house up by the mausoleum where I stayed at nights and slept there and lived my life for thirty-eight years. I got back from WWII in 1945, right after the treatise was signed after we'd dropped bombs on Hiroshima and Nagasaki and V-J Day got celebrated. My daddy had been a worker here at Summer Haven and I'd always helped out on summers and Saturdays when I didn't have to be at school, picking up trash and later running a lawnmower to make some money to buy me a car, but then the war came and I got drafted. When I got back Daddy had suffered a stroke and died, and there was a place vacant on the staff for someone, and since most of the men on the grounds crew had gone off to the service and moved on to other jobs and places, when I came back the cemetery offered me the job of permanent caretaker. I didn't have a whole lot of education and frankly wasn't wanting to acquire any more either, so I took the job mainly because they told me I could live in the caretaker's house for nothing and that way I wouldn't have to go home and live with my mother and sister. I knew if that ever got started I'd never get away until the both of them or me died, and I was ready to get out on my own right away. I didn't want to live or work anywhere where I had to take orders or follow a lot of rules.

I'd done enough of that for four years in the army already.

I was still a young man by then, and I was wanting to go out a lot at night, go down the road and drink beer at this bar called The What's Up, but after a year or two slaving my ass off during the day cutting yards and digging graves for upcoming funerals I got to where I'd knock off in the late afternoon and come back and eat frozen dinners or pot pies or sandwiches I bought from the grocery store a mile up the street and then lay there on my divan like I was a dead man myself and watch the TV that had been left behind by the caretaker before me. That TV was as old as me and I had to go through all kinds of twists and turns and arranging of the rabbit ears before I could get a picture clear enough to watch, and if I was to change stations I'd have to go through the whole procedure again, because the reception was different for all of them. I say all, but really there weren't but two when I started out, and after about ten years that had doubled to four, but it wasn't anything near to what people have today, where they can get about a thousand channels and not even move from their chair to change stations. I don't see how people can keep up with all they got and all the choices they have to make just to watch something.

Anyway, my habits all changed after a while, and except for a trip to the grocery store now and then I didn't ever do nothing much except work all day and then come home and eat and watch TV and get up every couple of hours or so and cruise around the grounds making sure nothing was going on, no kids carrying on Halloween tipping over tombstones or stealing them outright, no couples parking down any of the secluded paths making out or screwing, and no bunch of nuts meeting up to worship the devil at midnight or anything like that. That's what my job was, you know, to keep stuff like that from happening. That's why I got to live here in the cemetery all the time, to scare people off because they knew somebody would come across them sooner or later. I even bought myself a shotgun in case somebody got excited and tried to come at me when I came around. I figured having a shotgun would serve me well if I ever got outnumbered out here in the middle of the night, and I wasn't going to get myself hurt or killed protecting the place on the salary they paid me.

There's one thing a shotgun won't protect you from, though. Ghosts. There ain't a handgun or a rifle in the world that's able to do something about spirits. I could have my army-issued carbine with the telescopic sight and have a poltergeist dead-on in my eye and it wouldn't ever matter. A ghost you can't kill because they're already that way, and whether you want to think of me as crazy or not I'm still going to say that I've seen more than a few of them out at night and in the early morning stalking the grounds and floating around and appearing and disappearing, and I can tell you right now it's not a sight for the faint of heart. I saw dead guys a lot in the war so I know what a corpse looks like when they're not up and moving around, but there ain't a whole lot somebody can do when they're getting visited by one. It's a scary enough thing, I'll tell you the truth.

I don't think it was ever me these cemetery ghosts came to see. I didn't ever have one of them try to do me any harm. From all I ever saw it was almost like they knew who I was and why I was there and didn't wish to mess with me at all because they had other things to attend to. Mostly they just liked to move around and visit different places, sometimes they'd just drop by for a second and then before you knew it they'd be gone quick as a heartbeat, but the majority of the ones I came to be familiar with always seemed to show up at the same time in the same place, like they were re-membering something or the area they were in held some kind of importance to them. Most of the time they wouldn't fool with me at all, but would just hover or stand by a grave or a tree or maybe even take a seat on a nearby bench and ponder and meditate with-out making a sound. Not that they were all silent. There were a few that sang snatches of songs, or prayed really low, or cried for a time until it was time to leave. It was a busy place sometimes during the night hours. I could go out on my rounds and a lot of times it was like a gang of them were out there; other times I'd see nothing at all and wonder if all the other times I'd simply been imagining things. But I know what I saw. At first I wrote my sightings down in a notebook, but I never showed it to anybody. I also never said anything about it when I talked to any of my supervisors or the ground crew. I didn't want anybody thinking I was crazy and needed to be relieved of my job.

The first couple of years I was there I was still a pretty young guy, so it was hard to stay home every night out there by myself, especially when I started seeing apparitions on a nightly basis, so I got to where I would leave and go down the road and eat my dinner at a tavern and drink a few beers before heading back. I'd sit there at the bar and eat a steak sandwich or a cheeseburger and watch games on the overhead TV until I was politely polluted, then hop in the company pickup truck and head back to the cemetery. I was always careful not to drink too much so I wouldn't have a wreck or get pulled over on the way back, because I knew something like that would get my ass fired for sure, and I didn't want that. Sometimes I came mighty close to crossing the line, though.

There was this woman who worked in the cemetery office as a receptionist, so I got to where I'd see her pretty often when I came in to get my marching instructions for the day, and pretty soon we started talking and after that we started going out together. She was damn pretty and college-educated on top of that, and I started getting interested up to my neck before you knew it. We even started fooling around a good deal on our dates, and she came home with me out to the caretaker house sometimes, but she always said it creeped her out too much to spend the night. It got to where I'd go to her apartment and stay pretty late there, then leave and go back and inspect the grounds before hitting the sack. Everything was going along so good between us that I began thinking maybe I might pop the question sometime in the coming days and we could make it official. I was getting tired of living alone.

But things started going wrong between us before I knew it.

The big thing was Faye wasn't too interested in hearing my stories about the war or the dead people I'd seen there or my feelings about being around dead folks most of the time on my job. She wanted to go downtown to the taverns and dance and drink and have a big time every night and got to where she seemed bored with anything I suggested we do. She started hanging out with some of her old college friends a lot and pretty soon had made herself unavailable to spend any time with me. I'm not very pleased with the way I reacted, but the truth is I got pretty angry and obsessed about it and started trying to follow her wherever she went at night. I'd park by her apartment building and wait to see what she did, if she stayed home or went out alone or went off with her friends, which was bad enough either way because I wasn't involved, but soon I started seeing men coming by and taking her out on dates, and I didn't know whether to follow them and see where they went or go home and stew about it all night. With the way my temper was I decided the best thing to do was stop asking her out or calling or coming by the funeral home and catching her at her desk. I didn't know how it was it happened so fast, but I was in love and heartbroken and I knew in my head there was nothing I could ever do about it. Faye was gone from me for good, so I was going to have to learn to live with it.

I did stop coming around, which I guess pleased her, but I never was able to stop thinking about her. I saw her in my mind constantly and couldn't erase the image, and after a year or so I had grown so accustomed to always having the memory of her around that I gave up on the outside world and started living like a hermit. I was forty and except for my mother and my sister I didn't have any contact with anything or anyone outside the cemetery.

Even the cemetery employees all began avoiding me because I seemed so strange and distant. My mother died in 1956 and after she was gone I hardly left the grounds at all. I'd assign my crew their daily duties and I'd go around finishing up projects until it was time to lock the gates to try and keep people out, which was a pretty useless thing to do since there were two or three other ways to get in besides the front gates. I always found myself on the hill overlooking the funeral home watching Faye come out the door and walk to her car. I'd stand there until she drove away and then go home to my TV dinner. I'd drink my six-pack of Schlitz and then go stumbling out to do my evening rounds, getting in the truck and weaving up and down the main roads making sure nothing was going on.

Always during this final round I'd run into something that would throw me off my game and get me to feeling uneasy. Whether it was a buck or a doe with a fawn or a pack of coyotes on the hunt, it was like they would come at me from out of the darkness and give me a start with how quickly they appeared. Maybe I'd been around long enough that it wasn't that they scared me once I saw what was there, but it was the not knowing what was coming up on me that made me fearful. Like I said before, I'd seen things a lot spookier than the local wildlife out on the grounds, whether it be the black night when the clouds covered the moon and stars or the fog that rolled in off the river or the thick woods and shadows where who knows what might be lurking there. What I'm trying to say is there were ghosts in that cemetery then, just like there are ghosts roaming around out here now, and sometimes they don't want you to see them and sometimes they do, and it was many a time that I came across one of them that seemed to be wanting to speak to me to tell me something or just wanted me to see them and go away, but that was the way it was. And I don't mind saying that when I ran across one I did my best to go the other way and get out of its proximity, because I didn't want to have nothing to do with them. And I for sure didn't want them following me back to the house and taking up residence there. I couldn't have stayed there all those years if one of them had ever started doing something like that.

I caught wind that Faye had gotten engaged to some guy, and pretty soon she married and quit her job and moved away with him. I did my best not to think about it or listen to any of the details about her leaving, but I did learn that she and her new husband had moved to Baton Rouge, where he was going to be a schoolteacher there. By that time I knew I could kiss her goodbye forever.

The years went by and maybe I forgot her and maybe I didn't.

It was hard to say. Sometimes out of the blue the thought of her would come to me and I'd have a moment when I'd wonder how she was and if she was a mother or if she was happy, but most of the time I stayed busy working and watching television and drinking beer every night until I couldn't stand up, much less think, and so most of the time I was okay. It was like I'd descended into a void and nothing could get at me anymore. I was fine with having Faye come along as a passing thought, but I was glad that she wasn't the dominant subject in my mind anymore. I thought the way it was would make it easier for me to live out my life the rest of my days, with my memories of Faye and the War and the life I'd left behind all in their place in the past. I could remember them and ponder them a while, sure, but they were all so distant after a time that they didn't hold sway much anymore.

I never stopped seeing my visions though, call them ghostly visitations or apparition spottings or what, because those spirits seemed to be always out there and in my path on those nights and early mornings when I drove through the fog and the mist making sure what I was in charge of hadn't gone to hell overnight or some- time in the darkness. I'd see them out there right and left, some of them new and some familiar, and I got to the point I was pretty used to it. It was like not a bit of it scared me too much anymore.

But when I got up there in years I saw her again. Faye. One night when I came home from my final evening rounds she was there on the porch. It was all I could do to get around like I used to. For a long time I would park the truck at certain locations and walk around the sections to see what was going on, but as age overtook me it was easier to stay in the truck and strain my eyes from the passenger seat, and if something escaped me, well then, so be it. It wasn't like with my old age infirmities that I could have prevented a vandal from destroying property or a hooligan stealing a tombstone from a grave. Maybe it was just I'd grown tired of running across the spirits of the dead manifested in Summer Haven, and I had just as soon not view them anymore. Maybe I had experienced enough.

But on this night Faye rocked in my chair on the front porch.

I saw her from the truck and got out, but I was afraid to go up the steps to join her. I remembered how she had not wanted to see me again back those years ago. Had she changed her mind? Or was this my deluded imagination taking off on me again, perhaps this time for good. She did not look like I thought she would, like an old lady after all these years. She was as young as I remembered her.

And that is when I knew.

This was not a present-day Faye sitting in my chair waiting for me on my midnight porch. This was Faye of long-ago. Whether she was real or not I did not know.

I wondered if I should climb the stairs and say hello. Then I wondered why she was here and turned around to get back in the truck and drive away. Had she died and become a ghost herself, come back to Summer Haven to join in with all the other spirits? I decided after all this time I really didn't want to know. I thought it was better to leave those things in the darkness of the past alone. Whatever good there had been there for me was long-since gone.

I drove over to the funeral home and parked in the lot. I lit a cigarette and sat there looking at the streetlights and the clouds hiding the moon and stars. It looked like rain might be on the way.

I sat there for a minute or two more until the pain came up in my chest and I died. I was dead when they found me the next morning, but I wasn't all the way gone even then. I was still thinking about Faye sitting on my porch rocking away. It was like I couldn't get the image to leave me, not then or later, and I don't suppose it ever will.

# PEACEFUL VALLEY

## RUBY SCOTT SINGER
## (1925- 1967)
### Beloved Mother

Imet Paul Singer while we were both going to school at Wagner Green University in North Carolina after the War ended, in 1946 when I was a senior and he was in his second year of Divinity school getting his doctorate so he could become a Baptist preacher. At that time he was charming and handsome, an ex-football player who'd served two years in the Air Force during the war, and when he'd walked up to me one day as I was eating lunch in the cafeteria and asked me out I said yes immediately. He was a friend of one of my girlfriend's brother, and we'd met before at her parents' home when I'd come over for dinner. In a strange way I halfway thought that our meeting was one of those things that was meant to be.

I wasn't right about that, although it was a few years before I began to see the error of my ways. It was probably right about the seven year itch time in our marriage—after we had Wayne and Karen and had our house in Carter Heights and he'd been pastor of Brooks Hill Baptist Church a couple of years— that Paul started having affairs with some of the women in the church and around town who were married to his colleagues at other churches. He was very adept at it. No one knew about the duplicitous side of him he kept hidden from sight and the gift he possessed to have women come his way and make it appear it was all their idea to initiate the contact to begin with, therefore he was never beset with accusations and public confessionals from any of the women he was with because they were the ones who considered themselves to be at fault and he had been merely an innocent victim who'd fallen for their charms against his own will. It was only because one of these women came to me to ask for forgiveness that I came to discover that side of Paul at all. After the first glimpse into his covert actions, I was shocked at how many there had been before my suspicions became grounded. He'd been a busy boy.

My big mistake was not confronting him about his activities but keeping silent and deciding it was somehow my fault that all this had happened. I tried from that moment to be the perfect wife for him and hoped that by doing so it would cause him to cease in his ways and come back to our marriage where we could begin our relationship all over again. I believed that just because I was the mother of his two children I could use that and my feminine charms to draw Paul back to me again, that I was still the woman these years later who excited him the most and that his straying had been only an accident. I thought that if I reinvented myself and made more of an effort to be a lover on top of being a wife and mother then all would be well once more.

Needless to say, my plan didn't work. If anything, Paul's behavior seemed to multiply. It was as if he was gone all the time, inventing meetings he had to attend and out of town conferences where he had to be present for the sake of the church to keep it in good standing with the Baptist Convention. Maybe I believed it for a while longer, but the time finally came when I gave up hope and began worrying about what the future held for me. The more I tried to come up with a solution the more any rational answer eluded me.

It wasn't long before I began to imagine that everyone in my orb knew what was happening in our household. Being in a Southern Baptist church in a small town, it was difficult to decipher if the congregation had caught wind of what was going on and would soon drive us out of the church or if the membership would turn a blind eye to it all and pretend nothing was happening for the sake of upholding its reputation. I was torn between thinking I was harboring a terrible secret I was with-holding from everyone, or if everyone did indeed already know and was talking about me behind my back, whispers of pity and gossip and wondering if I was so intensely stupid that I did not know what was going on between my husband and the legions of women he was sleeping with. I was afraid to face any of them; I was afraid to open my mouth and speak the truth. For a long time I said and did nothing, allowing everything to contin-ue without interference from me. But all of it began mounting up inside me and the time came when it began to overwhelm me. I can't say I was thinking straight or I wouldn't have done anything to harm my children, but the truth is the reality of my situation clouded my rational thought and caused me to go into some sort of hysterical tunnel vision where all that existed was me out on some barren plain being left there by Paul, who was the only one who could come and rescue me but who I knew never would, because he was gone from me and with others and I was abandoned there in my horrible state of being and that was the way it was always going to be. It became my one and only train of thought. No matter what I did there would never be an escape from the fate that had befallen me. The more I tried to cope each day the more hopeless my situation became. Soon, the only thing that seemed important to me anymore was for it all to end.

I think back now and there are so many ways I could have chosen to dissolve the problem. I could have given Paul an ultimatum and had him leave the house under the threat I would make his actions public and destroy his career forever. I could have left with the children and gone somewhere else and left him alone in the church to face his congregation's scrutiny amid alimony and child support payments. I could have gone off alone and left the children in his care, which he would have hated because they would have cramped his style to no end, but I didn't do any of those balanced actions. I wasn't thinking clearly enough for that.

What I eventually did was begin going to bed earlier and earlier every night, going off to Sleepyville with the aid of Valium and Nervine washed down by a few gin and tonics. If Paul wasn't home but was out at one of his "meetings" I simply turned the television on in the den for the children to watch until they went to bed by themselves or until Paul came home and found them there. There were times when he didn't come home at all, and I would find them the next morning asleep in the floor or on the sofa with the television set still on, showing information shows or exercise programs for the housewife. They began missing school fairly regularly, but I was in another world and didn't take much notice. As long as I was in a heavy state of sedation I felt safe.

The night finally came around when I pushed the envelope to the limit. Everyone tried to smooth it over by saying it had been an accident on my part, which I was more than happy for people to believe such a thing, but now I know for certain it was not. It was intentional whether I want to confess to it or not, but it's long enough of a time now that there's no use in lying about it. The kids were staying over with Paul's parents that night, Paul was gone to a congregational pastors' meeting, and I was alone in the house. I sat down to watch some mindless television, but soon I wanted a drink, so I had one gin and tonic after another, not exactly the sort of pastime a Baptist preacher's wife should be indulging in on a Friday night. The more I drank the more the bad thoughts kept flooding in, so I turned to my medicine cabinet as usual to stick a finger in the dam. I wanted to turn everything off to relax and keep from thinking about what I knew I could do nothing about, so with every sip of gin I swallowed I added a pill to go with it. First a Valium, then some Nervine. Pretty soon I began to lose count.

The television and every light in the house was on when I went upstairs to bed. I remember how there were eleven steps up to the top of the stairway, then you made a slight left, and two more steps put you on the second floor. To the right was the kids' bedrooms, and down to the left was mine and Paul's. I was out of my mind but not so much that I wasn't afraid I'd start thinking about Paul if I got into our bed. I wasn't sure if I would hate him or miss him or both. But I was woozy and stumbling and I knew I could go no farther. I had to lie down.

After that, it was pretty much a blur. It's hard for me to say what was real and what wasn't, what was actually happening and what I was imagining. Dreaming. Hallucinating. I'd done quite a number on myself. I remember thinking about the possibility that I was never coming back from this realm of shadows and silence I'd entered into. Soon I didn't know whether I was imagining things or was indeed on the brink of death. Or maybe it was I was already dead but simply didn't know it yet. Maybe it's one of those things a person has to learn and experience before they understand their status between life and death.

I did die. Paul found me at some point in the early hours of the morning when he finally came home, and from what I remember I was still breathing when the ambulance team arrived. I remember hands working on me and being loaded into the back of the ambulance and rushed away with the siren shrieking, although by that time I wasn't certain if I was hanging on or had already passed over. It was hard to tell whether I was in the middle of it or was already somewhere else watching the entire process happen. I do remember when everyone stopped in their efforts to bring me back and save me, when the machines got turned off and the ER personnel left the room. That's when it started striking home that it was all over for me. I lay there in-between any emotions, which is strange when you think I was right then a newcomer to the afterlife, but the only feeling I could muster by then was just this state of being numb to it all.

Of course, Paul kept his head through those first moments after the nurses had covered me with a sheet and got busy making certain that it never came out publicly that his wife had committed suicide. Something like that would have ruined his ministry and his standing in the Baptist community. I don't know how he managed to do it or who he knew in high circles to stop such a scandal from getting out, but he managed it all right. There may have been a few people here and there who had some suspicions but there was never enough evidence around to prove anything. As far as the rest of the world was concerned I died as the result of an aneurism that had occurred instantaneously that no one had seen coming.

I know my children have never known any different from what got told to them. I guess if this was a full-fledged ghost story I could maybe appear before them like Prince Hamlet's father did and point them toward the truth, but I haven't been endowed with that kind of power yet. I have been able to in-filtrate Paul's dreams from time to time and cause him some moments of remorse, but it didn't stop him from re-marrying a year after I was gone to a woman ten years younger than I was. You'd think that somehow someone would see through this sham, but so far nobody has. People are blind on the most part. They only see what they want to see.

Speaking of my children, of course they're all grown up by now and have grown children and grandchildren of their own. Time doesn't stand still, even if I don't age anymore. I hardly know what to make of the both of them. They both come by here once or twice a year, maybe Mother's Day or Christ-mas mostly, but other than that I'm pretty certain I am nothing but an afterthought. The secret of my passing has been hidden from them for such a long while that I don't believe the idea of my death being a suicide even occurs in their heads these days, the same as it has always been since they were young and all of a sudden their mother was gone. Most of their memories have taken place with their father and the two subsequent wives he had after me.

Funny how things work out. Paul's first wife was a Jenni-fer who was twenty-five to his forty-four. I think he'd met her at the YMCA when he'd started using the treadmill on weekday mornings. I suppose they got accustomed to running side by side regularly, and one thing led to another. Like I say, it wasn't a year after I'd gone that she became the next Mrs. Singer, and it was another seven years before she died in a DUI accident. She was the one who was responsible, but luckily for Paul she was the only one who'd died and he picked up where he left off with me and turned that into a tragic accident too. He was the Poor Pastor Singer, who'd lost two wives in his life journey but still maintained his faith in God. I imagine after seven years good old Jennifer had begun to get a taste of Paul running around on her too, and I wouldn't doubt that was the reason she was out intoxicated by herself on a weekday night.

His last wife Melanie died of breast cancer two years ago. She was forty, almost as old as I was when I became history. I don't suppose Paul could be faulted for that, but at age forty I have a suspicion Melanie was on the verge of outliving her usefulness too.

Paul's still around these days, past eighty now if I've got it right, so I suppose his days of catting around are over by now, perhaps not mentally but physically for sure. After all this time I try and not think too ill of him, because there's a part of me that's glad I got away from him and all my misery when I did and it won't do me any good to wish bad things to happen to him at this point, like death, which face it, might be doing him a favor if it took him now. That to me seems much too charitable and something that wouldn't bring me much satisfaction or assure me of resting in peace from here on out. No, I think what I'd like for Paul is a lengthy spell of being old and disabled and decrepit, a chance to live for a while without those male powers he once possessed that he was always so proud of, but just a long term of doddering and being helpless and each day being unable to do anything for himself, to wet his pants and mess himself and maybe get a daily supply of baby food oozing down his throat. Maybe if that would happen and his mind would stay sharp enough for him to regret every hour he was still alive, then maybe that would be enough. I truly think God will forgive me for uttering such a small prayer, such a tiny thing in the way of revenge, because I'm certain He knows already what Paul Singer has stored up for himself in Paradise. Maybe if there's enough time Paul will come to know it too.

# CALVARY HILLS

## ELIZABETH MARIE CARLISLE
## (1949- )
## ONE OF A KIND

There's place for me right here beside Daddy and Mother when the time comes, but that day hasn't arrived yet. The Lord knows I'm ready, but I guess there are still some things left undone I need to deal with until the moment comes when I'm called to Heaven. I don't know when that's going to be or how it will come about, but I am ready when it happens. I've been preparing for it quite a long time now.

I guess it's been twenty-five years now since I had my cancer scare. I was diagnosed with breast cancer in my mid-forties, and at the time that was almost like being given a death sentence. I mean, people just didn't recover from such a thing back then the way they do now. I was in the middle of coming to terms with the fact that Barry and I were not together and probably never would be, so I was already right there at the end of my psychological rope, and then the doctor came at me with the devastating news that I'd tested positive and needed to begin undergoing treatment immediately. So, while I was trying to cope with my depression over Barry and me, I had to start undergoing radiation and chemo and finally had to have a mastectomy of my left breast, and after all that nobody was sure if it was all gone or not. That's when I turned to God with a litany of incessant prayer. To this day I'm convinced it was He who got me through it, not the doctors or surgeons or chemo or any of it. That's why I'm still so thankful and have never strayed from Him since.

I could have lost faith long before that though. I could have believed that God didn't love me at all or care whatsoever about what I was going through, and for a while that's exactly what happened. I lost the only man I ever loved because of an act of Satan, and I blamed God for allowing such a thing to happen. I know now that there are a lot of things that go on in this life we are living that are secondary to the Kingdom of Heaven and all Eternity that is to come. The lives we live on earth are but sprinkles of sand in comparison to the duration of the Everlasting Paradise we will come to know when God brings us into His presence.

It was drugs and the evil spirits of the world that took Barry away from me. We were together all through high school and I fully expected that when our college days were finished we would come together as man and wife and I would be at his side from then on until our deaths. I would teach on the college level and he would inherit his father's business—a Chevrolet/GM dealership—and after a time of getting his feet wet and his name known around the community he might transition into local politics as a councilman or a state senator, and from those positions move on to a higher office. Who knew the limit? Barry's father had been a judge, and he had an aunt who was a councilwoman and an uncle was considering making a run for the United States Senate. Barry was in position to rise in the ranks at some time in the future, and I would be the wife who would stand beside him and advise him when there were difficult decisions to be made.

So, Barry and I went to Knoxville after graduation and started on our way toward a golden future. I moved into a dorm and was accepted into Kappa Delta and everything was smooth, and for a while it was good for Barry too. He was accepted by Delta Kappa Epsilon, which was a fairly decent fraternity that a lot of the new boys were gravitating to, but it was there that Barry met some people who were soon to lead him down the wrong path and away from me. Before our first quarter had been completed Barry was missing classes and staying out all night with several of his new friends, and very soon it became almost impossible to locate him around campus anymore. He stopped calling me or meeting me for lunch or taking me out to dinner or the football games, and when he did come around it was usually just so he could take me out in his Camaro and find some motel or dead end where he could get his hands on me and get me undressed and do all sorts of things to me I'd never dreamed of before. Even when I got pregnant he didn't care, but just told me to deal with it myself and then disappeared. The next thing I knew he was gone from school and taken off to some unknown place in Texas or Louisiana or someplace—who knew? I certainly didn't, and neither did anyone in his family. As a matter of fact, his parents seemed to blame me for what was going on with him, like it was me who'd made him crazy and gotten him on drugs and caused him to run away. They didn't know about the illegal abortion I had and how I'd had to drop out of school too and come home to live with my parents, and how the only one who'd tried to understand was my daddy. My mother even got to the point that she thought of me as a whore, and even called me by that term once. It was as if my life was ruined and no one understood and I had to go off to some faraway place in my mind to learn how to deal with the cards that had been dealt me. For two years I basically stayed in my bedroom and waited for Barry to come back to me, and when he didn't and I knew he wasn't going to come back any time soon, I re-enrolled at a small Christian school and got my degree as originally planned, except now there was no Barry by my side and I was alone in my future undertakings.

I forgot to mention that my mother got lung cancer (she smoked like a chimney) and died during this time, so I had to deal with her death too on top of everything else.

I guess it's no wonder that I went a little strange during this period of my life, since it was like nothing good was going to stay within my reach and every time I turned around it seemed like something terrible would smack me in the face. Probably a lot of people would have been bitter and upset about such unfair moments happening to them and carried it with them for the rest of their lives, but I arrived at the conclusion that whatever was happening to me at the present time was only a test of my faith to see if I was worthy of the riches that would be coming my way later on, and so I thought of myself as a modern version of Job and I tried to maintain my faith as much as I could and learn patience and be secure in the thought that soon I would win out in this battle with the Devil and God would walk beside me in due time and for the rest of my life, and I am proud to say that is exactly what happened.

My faith in the Lord never wavered, no matter how many years passed and where each day took me. I got my teaching degree and landed a job teaching French at a community college, and that was okay for a while, because I was still living with Daddy and I didn't have many expenses to worry about. I was able to buy a new car—I got one of those big Sports Utility Vehicles that had big tires and set up really high so I could look down on the other cars in traffic, and so whenever it did snow and get icy I was one of the few that could always get to school or church and didn't have to stay at home and feel helpless. I guess I learned this from Daddy, to tell the truth. He had a big old truck too, had always had one for as long as I could recall, and he was always going and never stranded, so I suppose I wanted to be the same way too. I admired my daddy so much and got to where I wanted to be just like him, even if I was a girl, and if I couldn't be like him myself, I wanted a husband who was cut entirely from the same cloth. For a long time I thought Barry was that way, but Satan had taken Barry away before he had the chance to follow in Daddy's footsteps.

In a little while I managed to save up enough money to make a good down payment on a house, so I did that too. Daddy didn't really want me to move out, but by then I was getting close to forty and there was something inside me saying I needed to be out on my own. I was still harboring hopes that Barry was going to come back to me one day, and I wanted to make certain the two of us had a place where we could be together with no interference from anyone else.

I'd kept up with Barry's comings and goings over the years. After he'd left school I learned he'd gone out west to Albuquerque and lived there for a while, going to school for a year or so at a community college before dropping out and coming back home. Somehow or another he managed to stay out of the draft (probably because of his asthma, he always suffered from asthma) and his dad got him a couple of jobs to tide him through. He sold cars for a while, then went through a stint as an insurance agent, and then worked for an athletic store selling sports equipment, shoes and jerseys and caps and such. He changed jobs a lot and disappeared from the scene often, so as much as I tried keeping up with him there were times when it was all just a blank space. He'd be back to drinking and taking drugs and laying up in places and never showing his face. I wasn't much for attending school reunions, because my classmates all liked to see me in my single state and then talk about me later behind my back, but I went anyway because it afforded me the means to find out the latest on what Barry was doing, if anyone had seen him or knew what his life was like. I found out at the twenty-fifth anniversary gathering that he had married a woman whose father had worked at the courthouse with Barry's dad, and the two of them were living a county away in a house owned by her family. She was working for the state and had been for years, but nobody seemed to know what Barry was doing.

I was the one to find out, because he called me out of the blue one night, drunk and high and very blue. He told me how his life had gone to shit and how I was the only girl in the world he had ever loved and how he'd regretted every day the way he'd left me behind. It was the drugs and the alcohol that did it, he said. It wasn't you. I just had a lot of problems back then and I didn't know how to cope. I thought the best thing I could do was to go off by myself for a while and solve my troubles that way, not put you or anyone else through it, but just to go away until I had my head together. Well, it's taken a long time, he said, but I think I'm back now. I'm ready to start leading a new life. And that's why I'm calling you.

A lot of people would call me a fool and tell me I never should have believed anything he told me, but the thing of it is I know Barry and understand how hard it is to trust anyone or face up to life when it came his way, because he wasn't given the opportunity as a child to learn those things. He had no one to help him along. His mother was dead and gone and his father had never tried to be helpful or provide any kind of example for Barry to follow. It was as if he had been left alone at an early age to figure out everything for himself, and he had never had the knowledge or experience within him to resolve the situation. Sometimes he'd chosen the wrong path because he didn't have anyone to advise him and didn't know better on his own. The rest of the world may have faulted him for his mistakes and behavior, but I certainly didn't back then and hadn't done so anytime over the years.

See, the thing of it is that after all was said and done and whatever bad event had happened I still knew that Barry loved me the entire time while it was going on. I never questioned it one time. When he went away I knew he'd be back someday. When I heard he'd married someone else I knew even through the hurt that he'd made a mistake and it would rectify itself one day. I had no doubt in my mind that God had blessed our union right from the very beginning and that it was only a matter of time before it would come to be the way He'd ordained it. I even accepted the fact that the two of us might never come together in this world but would have to wait until we'd crossed the threshold of life and were together in Heaven before the Throne of God before our union was complete. Once I accepted this revelation, I was content with waiting during this sojourn on earth. I knew that God had a plan for us, and at some time in the future when this short session on earth was done the two of us would be together in Paradise.

It's good I held the faith I did because things did not go well when Barry and I met again. He was not ready to be bathed in the light of God yet, but was still under the spell of Evil and Satan, and on our first meeting it was clear he wanted nothing but carnalities between us again and nothing more, and I sinned in allowing him such. He even told me was never coming back to me for as long as we both lived, that I was a fool now and had always been one, and how he couldn't stand to look at me anymore, much less be in bed with me, because there was something about me that sickened him now even more than it once did.

And then he left me crying in my new house, wanting to grab my keys and go to Daddy. But I knew God sometimes worked in unusual ways and maybe this was one of them. I knew if I had faith in God and was patient, all things would be answered in time.

I didn't know anything about Barry for a while. He never called me back, but I learned in the paper that his wife's mother had died and he was not listed as one of the survivors, so I knew by that they had divorced. I didn't know where Barry was until three years after that, when I saw his death notice in the obituaries. All it said was his full name and the city and state, no arrangements or services scheduled. Somehow I knew he'd be cremated and I would never know where his ashes had been placed. The good thing about that was that God came to me in a dream and comforted me and told me that Barry's ashes would find me when the day came for me to cross over and be buried here in my plot, that he would come to me in time.

I've had peace since that time. I know my earthly voyage will end in due time, whenever it is God wills to call me home, and I know that when that time comes Barry and I will be reunited, like that song Diana Ross sang, that someday we'll be together, and then everything will be as God has promised me.

I don't doubt things or question things anymore. I trust in God and go about my daily life. I've stopped teaching school and don't go to church much anymore except for Christmas and Easter and on Barry's birthday, and I read my Bible and say my prayers and feed my canary, a yellow little bird who sings to me while I cook my meals. Most mornings now I come out here to Summer Haven to visit Mother and Daddy and just sort of stand here where I'll be with them one day soon. I think of how peaceful it will be when Mother and Daddy and Barry and I will all be together for eternity, when the day comes when we'll all be gathered up to go to Heaven. It gives great comfort to me.

I only wish that day would come, but I tell myself to not worry, to be patient, because God's plan is yet to be set in action. I wake each morning and wonder if this day will be my last, if soon I'll be with Barry here in our place, and all the tribulations Satan placed before us are gone from us forever. Amen, I say to that. I pray to God His will be done.

# SUMMER HAVEN
## (1783- )

There more souls abiding here you don't know about. In all your time walking through these grounds you have still only scratched the surface. There are more stories longing to be heard, more voices crying out. No one ever has the time to disclose everything. No one gets to tell it all.

The farther one gets from the entranceway with the sign that says Summer Haven Cemetery and Burial Grounds, on past the stone wall and the first long garden leading to the funeral home and the lot where the hearses are parked to the expanse of the twelve sections housing the twenty-nine areas of plots housing the families and the veterans and the historical markers, all the way past where the Peace and Garden Mausoleums sit by the trees that lead to the cliff that overlooks the interstate, one finds themself in a world apert from noise and bustle. One becomes immersed in a world set apart where visitation will someday be followed by dwelling here for eternity.

Men and women, boys and girls, heroes and villains. Coffins and urns, bones and dust. History gathered here together. Some dead and gone and forgotten before others were even conceived, come here from differing statures and neighborhoods and postures, joined here now in the common bond of death, to reside here longer than they ever once walked the earth.

How long they stay around has never been said; where they travel from here remains a mystery. There is no answer to the question of whether what accomplishments were carried out during their thin existences will ever make a difference in the vastness of time yet to come. All the waiting and the reposing in the spin of the endless rotation of the planet will never provide a solution. The people were born and lived out there somewhere in the air and the light and the darkness that ended each day, and then the time came for them to be gone and become a part of the legion of the dead, to rest in peace or uneasily in regret, to repose in fading memory or to be immediately forgotten and be said good riddance to, to fade in being and memory and thought, to be in this country of their own surrounded by the others who came before or with them or will follow along in the hereafter.

This is the place where the dead come to take their next step. Neither they or the living who come to visit here know what that next realm will be, where the pathway leads them.

# EPILOGUE

It's like this just about every time I take a walk through this place. You'd think that after all this time I'd be used to the scene by now and not all the while during one of my excursions get myself dragged off into some room of my consciousness and have to hear another story from one of the restless leftover spirits who dwell here. It's like even though they're dead and gone they still can't leave because they're trying to work something out that happened before they had time to resolve it. You'd think that they'd give it up once they realize it's all behind them now, but it seems that's not the case. It's like they're determined to get it right or at least come to some understanding of why everything turned out for them the way that it did.

You know, I've got a few of my kinfolk out here myself, but I haven't had any of them up and strike up a conversation with me yet. I keep expecting it. My mother and father are here, but I suspect they're all out of words to try and tell me anything, because they know all of what they said to me fell on deaf ears for a long time a long way back. It wasn't that we had a tempestuous relationship going on between us the whole time, but mostly that they lived in their world and I lived in mine. It wasn't really anybody's fault. It was just the way it goes sometimes, nothing too strange about it at all.

My big sister, Olivia, always stayed close to my folks. She was their favorite because she never caused them any trouble. She was a straight arrow for sure. She started dating her husband Johnny in her sophomore year of high school and they married when they graduated college together and offered up three grandchildren for my parents to enjoy, while I ran around with a bunch of guys who liked drinking beer and smoking dope and seeing how many girls we could screw. I didn't really get into trouble, but I didn't bring much joy to them either. Like I say, we kind of lived in different worlds most of the time.

By the way, Johnny died a couple of years ago—he's down in a section close to the road—but I haven't had him say anything to me so far. We never were really that close, so it's understandable. Maybe he speaks to Olivia. I don't know.

I always knew about one set of my grandparents who are planted here, but I don't give them much thought very often, because the truth is my grandfather died when I was two and my grandmother checked out about a year or so after that, so the thing is I don't remember them much at all. These two were my mother's parents, so what I did know about them came from those Easters and Mother's Days and Christmases when Mama would have everybody load up in the car after church and come and deck their gravesite with whatever decorations the holiday called for, wreaths or artificial flowers or this painted Styrofoam cross Mama liked to display there from Maundy Thursday through Easter Sunday. I ran across that damn thing in the attic after Mama died and we were getting the place ready for an estate sale. There it was all wrapped up in a plastic bag like it was something precious, yellow and pink with this white lace border that even the birds flying around the cemetery wouldn't care to shit upon. I started to throw it away and be done with it, but then I decided to run an experiment to see if anybody was nuts enough to buy it. I came back the last day of the sale just to see, and sure enough, it was gone. I just shook my head. Somebody buying that cross pretty well sums up the way I feel about the human race. A person could take a crap in a bag and you could bet the ranch there'd be somebody who'd come along and buy it.

Myself, I finally did get married on up in my middle thirties, but by that time most all my family except for my sister and her kids were dead already, so there wasn't much use on my end planning any kind of big ceremony so everybody could come and celebrate at the big miracle of me finally finding some woman dumb enough to marry me. It turned out that Sherry had enough family members of her own to make up a big enough roster of folks for a wedding, so I found myself surrounded by her family and friends and a bunch of women from her college sorority she used for her bridal party. I was so bereft I had to use her brother for a Best Man, since practically all of my friends lived out of state and we weren't very close anymore anyway, so I didn't feel like asking anybody to travel a long way just for that one day, especially when it was sort of an unspoken fact I had in my head that this whole marriage thing wasn't going to be one of those eternal to death do you part sort of things. In the brutal reality portion of my brain I gave it five years tops.

I was close. I made it nine years just from extra effort and knowing also I'd only have one kid to pay support on and no alimony because the breaking up had been mostly Sherry's idea. I did agree to it though.

So, somebody might ask, why would a guy go through with something this life-altering and serious if he thought it wasn't something God had blessed in Heaven and wanted to see happen? I suppose the reason is I was about the only guy I knew who wasn't married by then, and maybe I felt like I was calling attention to myself as standing out as a weirdo. I'd caught myself getting bored drinking like a fish every night in my solitary apartment or cruising bars trying to look interesting enough that some woman would talk to me. Nothing like that had ever happened too frequently before, and it certainly wasn't happening later either, because the truth was I was getting too damn old for the scene. Plus, I wasn't the least bit interested in going through the motions anymore.

I got to know Sherry because we were both employed at Grandview Realty together. She was running the office and I was the property manager, driving around in a van all day towing a riding mower and nursing a hangover from the night before. I'd gotten my B.S. degree thinking maybe I'd go into some kind of business one day, but for twelve years I'd been painting and cutting yards and getting new houses ready to go on the market, performing manual labor because I didn't really want to be stuck somewhere taking orders all day. I had houses to tidy up for a good portion of the day, but most of the time I just parked somewhere and went into places and ate lunch and downed a couple of beers and then took cat naps and rode around in the van listening to sports talk shows on the radio. Sometimes I'd come back to the office and shoot the bull with Sherry, mainly because at the time she had the best legs of all the other female realtors and wasn't married, so after a period of flirting I zeroed in on her. Maybe she zeroed in on me, I don't know. I think the way it came down was both of us were eager to change our life one way or another.

We dated and hung around each other for close to two years, then she started acting like it was time for us to decide about whether we were ever going to go to another level and get married or not. I was kind of fifty-fifty on the whole idea, a part of me didn't care one way or another, but I decided to go ahead and propose and get it out of the way just so I wouldn't start thinking about being in the minority anymore. I figured with the way we were almost always together all the time anyway then we might as well make it legal, and when Sherry got pregnant I think both of us decided it was as good a time as any to tie the knot.

Like the way I've always been with just about everything, I didn't hate it or love it being married to Sherry and having a kid and being a father but was simply sort of in-between the whole time, some of it good and some of it bad, but I was good at adjusting at least, so I never was altogether miserable the entire nine years. The funny thing is, while I wasn't the ideal husband during our time together, Sherry was a hell of a lot worse than me as far as acting like a married person. I'll bet she cheated on me three or four times before I ever did anything to that effect—she was screwing other teachers and guys and even had a little fling with the assistant principal at our kid's school, which got him fired and we had to transfer our son Jason to another school, while at least I had sense enough to keep what I was doing undercover and not get too far in over my head at any time. Of course, when it came time for us to split up she made it look like I was the bad guy and she was the Virgin Frigging Mary and it needed to be me who paid out the nose for child support and alimony. Luckily, we had a judge who saw through her act some and thought she might be even creepier than I was, and so in the long run everything got split up fairly equally. Sherry got custody of Jason, which was okay by me, because the last thing in the world I wanted was to be burdened by having a kid at home keeping me from going and doing what I wanted, so I was glad to pay support and let Sherry have him. So, after all that, I became a divorced father, which as far as standards go in the world these days, made me a pretty normal guy.

My dad's parents—my paternal grandparents—are just a little down from my parents, so I see them pretty often. I never get any particular vibe when I pass by, like there was some connection between us or anything, probably because both of them were dead before I ever even came along. Grandad fell off a pier on a Florida fishing trip and got swept out into the Gulf by a rip tide or something, and by the time they located him six or seven hours later he was drowned bigger than hell. This was five years before I was born, and then a couple of months before my mother went into labor with me my grandmother dropped dead of a stroke while she was cooking herself breakfast on Thanksgiving morning. I never found out whether the family was supposed to come to her house for dinner that day or not, but I do know my dad never was a big fan of turkey anytime I was growing up.

So, the thing of it is I was never close to any of my grandparents whether they were alive or dead, and in my mind I know it wouldn't have made any difference if the timing was reversed and one set was alive and the other dead, because the results would have been the same. I was the grandson no one knew either in life or death. I was the one that didn't draw attention either way, so it was hard for any of them to remember me whatsoever. And vice versa.

It makes me wonder sometimes. Mostly the thought comes into my head whenever I come by here for one of my walks. I pass by and I see all these tombstones with names and dates on them and for a little while during my stroll I'll think about the people I did know that I'm passing by and I'll think about the ones I didn't, and a lot of times a story will come into my head about what really happened that I knew of and what might have happened that I wasn't involved in. It comes to me how everybody has a life they live and when it's over people either remember them or they don't, depending on what took place while that person was living. I think how sometimes people just go through their lives doing nothing special, drawing no notice from the world they're passing through, and then they're stuck out here in the ground and buried here in all their inconsequential lack of splendor and that's the way it's going to stay for eternity. And a lot of times I wonder if that's the way it's going to be for me too.

Because, let's face it, I haven't really set the woods on fire anytime yet in my life, and I'm beginning to recognize that my time for blazing out a glorious legacy is probably far behind me these days. I'm not so certain I have the capacity of wonder and enthusiasm contained in me anymore so that I have the energy to make a dent in the big humdrum wall that surrounds the ordinary and mundane with no color in their cheeks or spice in their imagination. I'm starting to think I am one of those rank and file born with no zeal or spark in their bones, who come to realize when it's too late that a parade has passed them by and they were too disinterested to join it. I'm thinking maybe I was too busy trying to keep from making any kind of effort to get through the day and did nothing at all in my allotted time, and now there's nothing to do but watch from a distance and deliberate on things that might have been.

These are not happy thoughts to dwell on. I envision how it may be in another decade or so, when my sister comes by with her kids to visit her parents, and how she'll point over to where I am and say that's where your uncle is. Uncle Ben. I don't guess you remember him. Or it could be Sherry coming by here with my own son, bringing him by to show him where his dad is because after so long a time he finally wondered enough to ask. All anyone will see is my name and some dates, which probably won't be enough to distinguish me from any of the other drab personalities buried around me. The way I see it is that when that day comes there'll be nothing for anyone to take away other than knowing where I am. There's nothing else to give them but that.

Unpleasant thoughts. I seem to be getting them more often these days.

I generally take an hour for lunch most days, and I generally leave the office and go through a takeout line and carry my lunch over here to Summer Haven. I keep a lawn chair in the back of my SUV, and if it isn't raining or cold as hell I'll sometimes sit under a tree and eat and listen to the wind blow with the words in my head providing accompaniment. I guess it's taken me an inordinate amount of time—decades at last count—to somewhat get my head together where I don't let my dissatisfaction with life and my abiding disappointment with my own history get in the way like it used to. When my first marriage went to pot and I was constantly at that stage where I told myself I was nothing but a failure and repeated the fact day after day until it was like a mantra, I finally arrived at a place where I could see I wasn't as bad as I had made out for so long. It was being here at Summer Haven where I could see the lives of others around me, and it didn't take a stroke of genius to realize that all who were resting here had gone through their shares of ups and downs too, before me, and except for the few cases where a life was ended by a bullet or a leap off a bridge or an automobile crash at high speed or some other instantaneous departure, there wasn't much difference in the majority of Summer Haven's dead and its daily visitor, me. There was good and bad in the world enough for everyone, so perhaps I shouldn't take things so personally.

In that sense, I suppose I've learned a few important things by my regular attendance here. Maybe the most important thing is I am not so much alone as I was for years. Not anymore. I feel I am part of some legion here, the dead linked with the living, and it just might be that the dead get as much comprehension of what the universe is all about just by seeing me arrive each day. Perhaps my presence provides some sort of link to what they have left behind, that maybe it makes them remember what living was like no matter how long ago it was, and it could be by remembrance they can come to terms with whatever great and grave consequence has followed them into the afterlife and disrupted their peace. I like to think that the departed and I are constantly learning from each other.

I actually have somewhat of a life these days. I am in a relationship with a woman who attends church where I do. Yes, I went back to church this past year, mostly to combat the emptiness of Sunday mornings with the television and too many cups of pondering coffee. I walked into a Methodist church with no prior knowledge of what I would encounter, and now after a couple of months I am friends with new people and have been introduced at a church luncheon to a lady who is once-divorced like me. I don't know how this will go—we do not know each other well-enough yet for it to be unbearable in our proximity to each other, so that is good. I tell myself to simply plod on, and if this doesn't work out there are other avenues to travel. This, I tell myself, is what it is like to be alive. The temperatures change, the sun comes up and then goes down, there's rain and shine and fog and snow. The world is always spinning. Every day is a new one.

And so I tell myself that here where I'm standing are stories rich in abundance, mine included, and that these stories are enough to keep a listener or a viewer enthralled for a lifetime until they and I become a member of the chorus too. And here in our little corner of the world, in our inconsequential town and our petty, insignificant histories, there are tales and stories that enthrall and entertain and teach the lessons learned from a lifetime, and all this goes on further and larger as it spreads from place to place, city to state, to all the final destinations in the world.

The dead are omnipotent and everlasting, among us even after they have departed and gone to other realms. A part of them is gone while a fragment of dust remains behind, speaking and crying out, waiting for whatever comes next, watching the world go by and wondering what it was and is and what in god's name it has been all about.

Waiting, just like I am, for an answer.

# END

**www.powderriverpublishing.com**